## FROM THE INFINITE NIGHT OF SPACE CAME . . . THE INTRUDER!

It took them an hour to carry out the elaborate preflight routine. But when they were done, they knew the ship was secure for takeoff. There was neither contraband cargo nor any stowaways on board. All systems were go, and they had made it with ten minutes to spare.

Two hours later, the last course correction that the tracking stations on Earth could give them had been fed into the computer. From now on they were on their own. There were just the three of them here—and no one else within a million miles.

In the circumstances, the detonation of an atomic bomb could hardly have been more shattering than the modest knock on the cabin door. . . .

*—from "Refugee"*

# The Other Side of the Sky

**by ARTHUR C. CLARKE**

**24 short stories of the future**

A SIGNET BOOK

NEW AMERICAN LIBRARY

TIMES MIRROR

## TO HECTOR

Published by arrangement with Harcourt Brace Jovanovich

 SIGNET TRADEMARK REG. U.S. PAT. OFF. AND FOREIGN COUNTRIES
REGISTERED TRADEMARK—MARCA REGISTRADA
HECHO EN CHICAGO, U.S.A.

SIGNET, SIGNET CLASSICS, MENTOR, PLUME, MERIDIAN AND NAL BOOKS *are published by The New American Library, Inc., 1633 Broadway, New York, New York 10019*

FIRST SIGNET PRINTING, NOVEMBER, 1959

9   10   11   12   13   14   15   16   17

PRINTED IN THE UNITED STATES OF AMERICA

These stories were written during the period 1947-1957, and with the three earlier collections, *Expedition to Earth, Reach for Tomorrow,* and *Tales from the White Hart,* complete the roster of my pre-Space Age fiction.

I have thrice—to my knowledge, that is—written stories based on ideas provided by someone else. My friends will testify that I am too sober a person to have imagined "No Morning After," which was due to A. H. Smith, while "All the Time in the World" springs from the multifarious talents of Mike Wilson. In 1953, I turned the latter tale into a television play, which was broadcast over the American Broadcasting Company network. Since then I have avoided any permanent entanglements with TV, though a purely social contact with the late "Captain Video" was undoubtedly responsible for "Security Check."

"The Nine Billion Names of God" was the product of a rainy afternoon in New York; Professor J. B. S. Haldane once challenged the mathematical basis of the title, but it's still a nice number.

"Refugee," to the utter confusion of indexers, was first published by Anthony Boucher in *The Magazine of Fantasy and Science Fiction* as "?," since he found my original title unsatisfactory and promptly started a competition to find a better one, finally settling upon "This Earth of Majesty." To add to the chaos, Ted Carnell, in the British magazine *New Worlds,* called it "Royal Prerogative."

"The Star" has a somewhat unusual history. In 1954, Carl Biemiller of *Holiday* magazine asked me to write an astronomical article, which I tackled with some reluctance because it involved a considerable amount of research (*i.e.,* work). It proved well worth it, however, because after publication in *Holiday* the piece concerned—whose title I won't mention, because it would give away the plot—was picked by *Reader's Digest.* Then the London *Observer* announced a short-story competition on the subject "2500 AD," and I realized that I had a theme already to hand. The story was written in a state of unusually intense emotion; needless to say, it wasn't even placed among the "also rans." As some compensation, however, on its eventual magazine appearance "The Star" was voted the best science-fiction story of 1956.

"Venture to the Moon" also has an unusual genesis. It was written as a series of six independent but linked stories for the London *Evening Standard,* and when the commission was first proposed I turned it down. It appeared impossible to write stories in only 1,500 words which would be understandable to a mass readership despite being set in a totally alien environment, but on second thought this seemed such an interesting challenge that I decided to tackle it. The resulting series was successful enough to demand a second, "The Other Side of the Sky," which by good luck appeared on the London newsstands just when Sputnik I appeared in the sky.

The short story "Take a Deep Breath" has been strongly criticized because of its suggestion that an unprotected man could survive in the vacuum of space. Experiments with dogs and chimpanzees (which have suffered no ill-effects after *three minutes* in vacuum) have now completely validated this idea. Stanley Kubrick later used it in one of the most dramatic sequences from *2001: A Space Odyssey.*

I must admit that "The Starting Line" has already been by-passed by history; there will probably be Russians and Americans on the moon before the first Englishman gets into orbit. But "Watch This Space" describes a phenomenon now seen by millions of people along the eastern seaboard of the United States; only a few days ago I watched a glowing flower of light unfold in the Washington sky, as one of the Wallops Island research rockets dumped a few pounds of barium into the ionosphere. So it is doubtless now only a matter of time before the advertising agencies move into space. . . .

ARTHUR C. CLARKE

# CONTENTS

## THE NINE BILLION NAMES OF GOD

"THIS IS a slightly unusual request," said Dr. Wagner, with what he hoped was commendable restraint. "As far as I know, it's the first time anyone's been asked to supply a Tibetan monastery with an Automatic Sequence Computer. I don't wish to be inquisitive, but I should hardly have thought that your—ah—establishment had much use for such a machine. Could you explain just what you intend to do with it?"

"Gladly," replied the lama, readjusting his silk robes and carefully putting away the slide rule he had been using for currency conversions. "Your Mark V Computer can carry out any routine mathematical operation involving up to ten digits. However, for our work we are interested in *letters*, not numbers. As we wish you to modify the output circuits, the machine will be printing words, not columns of figures."

"I don't quite understand. . . ."

"This is a project on which we have been working for the last three centuries—since the lamasery was founded, in fact. It is somewhat alien to your way of thought, so I hope you will listen with an open mind while I explain it."

"Naturally."

"It is really quite simple. We have been compiling a list which shall contain all the possible names of God."

"I beg your pardon?"

"We have reason to believe," continued the lama imperturbably, "that all such names can be written with not more than nine letters in an alphabet we have devised."

"And you have been doing this for three centuries?"

"Yes: we expected it would take us about fifteen thousand years to complete the task."

"Oh," Dr. Wagner looked a little dazed. "Now I see why you wanted to hire one of our machines. But exactly what is the *purpose* of this project?"

The lama hesitated for a fraction of a second, and Wagner wondered if he had offended him. If so, there was no trace of annoyance in the reply.

"Call it ritual, if you like, but it's a fundamental part of our belief. All the many names of the Supreme Being—God, Jehovah, Allah, and so on—they are only man-made labels. There is a philosophical problem of some difficulty here, which I do not propose to discuss, but somewhere among all the possible combinations of letters that can occur are what one may call the *real* names of God. By systematic permutation of letters, we have been trying to list them all."

"I see. You've been starting at AAAAAAA . . . and working up to ZZZZZZZZ. . . ."

"Exactly—though we use a special alphabet of our own. Modifying the electromatic typewriters to deal with this is, of course, trivial. A rather more interesting problem is that of devising suitable circuits to eliminate ridiculous combinations. For example, no letter must occur more than three times in succession."

"Three? Surely you mean two."

"Three is correct: I am afraid it would take too long to explain why, even if you understood our language."

"I'm sure it would," said Wagner hastily. "Go on."

"Luckily, it will be a simple matter to adapt your Automatic Sequence Computer for this work, since once it has been programed properly it will permute each letter in turn and print the result. What would have taken us fifteen thousand years it will be able to do in a hundred days."

Dr. Wagner was scarcely conscious of the faint sounds from the Manhattan streets far below. He was in a different world, a world of natural, not man-made, mountains. High up in their remote aeries these monks had been patiently at work, generation after generation, compiling their lists of meaningless words. Was there any limit to the follies of mankind? Still, he must give no hint of his inner thoughts. The customer was always right. . . .

"There's no doubt," replied the doctor, "that we can modify the Mark V to print lists of this nature. I'm much more worried about the problem of installation and maintenance. Getting out to Tibet, in these days, is not going to be easy."

"We can arrange that. The components are small enough to travel by air—that is one reason why we chose your machine. If you can get them to India, we will provide transport from there."

"And you want to hire two of our engineers?"

"Yes, for the three months that the project should occupy."

"I've no doubt that Personnel can manage that." Dr. Wagner scribbled a note on his desk pad. "There are just two other points—"

Before he could finish the sentence the lama had produced a small slip of paper.

"This is my certified credit balance at the Asiatic Bank."

"Thank you. It appears to be—ah—adequate. The second matter is so trivial that I hesitate to mention it—but it's surprising how often the obvious gets overlooked. What source of electrical energy have you?"

"A diesel generator providing fifty kilowatts at a hundred and ten volts. It was installed about five years ago and is quite reliable. It's made life at the lamasery much more comfortable, but of course it was really installed to provide power for the motors driving the prayer wheels."

"Of course," echoed Dr. Wagner. "I should have thought of that."

The view from the parapet was vertiginous, but in time one gets used to anything. After three months, George Hanley was not impressed by the two-thousand-foot swoop into the abyss or the remote checkerboard of fields in the valley below. He was leaning against the wind-smoothed stones and staring morosely at the distant mountains whose names he had never bothered to discover.

This, thought George, was the craziest thing that had ever happened to him. "Project Shangri-La," some wit back at the labs had christened it. For weeks now the Mark V had been churning out acres of sheets covered with gibberish. Patiently, inexorably, the computer had been rearranging letters in all their possible combinations, exhausting each class before going on to the next. As the sheets had emerged from the electromatic typewriters, the monks had carefully cut them up and pasted them into enormous books. In another week, heaven be praised, they would have finished. Just what obscure calculations had convinced the monks that they needn't bother to go on to words of ten, twenty, or a hundred letters, George didn't know. One of his recurring nightmares was that there would be some change of plan, and that the high lama (whom they'd naturally called Sam Jaffe, though he didn't look a bit like him) would suddenly announce that the project would be extended to approximately A.D. 2060. They were quite capable of it.

George heard the heavy wooden door slam in the wind as Chuck came out onto the parapet beside him. As usual, Chuck was smoking one of the cigars that made him so popular with the monks—who, it seemed, were quite willing to embrace all the minor and most of the major pleasures of life. That was one thing in their favor: they might be crazy, but they weren't bluenoses. Those frequent trips they took down to the village, for instance . . .

"Listen, George," said Chuck urgently. "I've learned something that means trouble."

"What's wrong? Isn't the machine behaving?" That was the worst contingency George could imagine. It might delay his return, and nothing could be more horrible. The way he felt now, even the sight of a TV commercial would seem like manna from heaven. At least it would be some link with home.

"No—it's nothing like that." Chuck settled himself on the parapet, which was unusual because normally he was scared of the drop. "I've just found what all this is about."

"What d'ya mean? I thought we knew."

"Sure—we know what the monks are trying to do. But we didn't know *why*. It's the craziest thing—"

"Tell me something new," growled George.

"—but old Sam's just come clean with me. You know the way he drops in every afternoon to watch the sheets roll out. Well, this time he seemed rather excited, or at least as near as he'll ever get to it. When I told him that we were on the last cycle he asked me, in that cute English accent of his, if I'd ever wondered what they were trying to do. I said, 'Sure'—and he told me."

"Go on: I'll buy it."

"Well, they believe that when they have listed all His names—and they reckon that there are about nine billion of them—God's purpose will be achieved. The human race will have finished what it was created to do, and there won't be any point in carrying on. Indeed, the very idea is something like blasphemy."

"Then what do they expect us to do? Commit suicide?"

"There's no need for that. When the list's completed, God steps in and simply winds things up . . . bingo!"

"Oh, I get it. When we finish our job, it will be the end of the world."

Chuck gave a nervous little laugh.

"That's just what I said to Sam. And do you know what happened? He looked at me in a very queer way, like I'd been stupid in class, and said, 'It's nothing as trivial as *that*.'"

George thought this over for a moment.

"That's what I call taking the Wide View," he said presently. "But what d'you suppose we should do about it? I don't see that it makes the slightest difference to us. After all, we already knew that they were crazy."

"Yes—but don't you see what may happen? When the

list's complete and the Last Trump doesn't blow—or whatever it is they expect—*we* may get the blame. It's our machine they've been using. I don't like the situation one little bit."

"I see," said George slowly. "You've got a point there. But this sort of thing's happened before, you know. When I was a kid down in Louisiana we had a crackpot preacher who once said the world was going to end next Sunday. Hundreds of people believed him—even sold their homes. Yet when nothing happened, they didn't turn nasty, as you'd expect. They just decided that he'd made a mistake in his calculations and went right on believing. I guess some of them still do."

"Well, this isn't Louisiana, in case you hadn't noticed. There are just two of us and hundreds of these monks. I like them, and I'll be sorry for old Sam when his lifework backfires on him. But all the same, I wish I was somewhere else."

"I've been wishing that for weeks. But there's nothing we can do until the contract's finished and the transport arrives to fly us out."

"Of course," said Chuck thoughtfully, "we could always try a bit of sabotage."

"Like hell we could! That would make things worse."

"Not the way I meant. Look at it like this. The machine will finish its run four days from now, on the present twenty-hours-a-day basis. The transport calls in a week. O.K.—then all we need to do is to find something that needs replacing during one of the overhaul periods—something that will hold up the works for a couple of days. We'll fix it, of course, but not too quickly. If we time matters properly, we can be down at the airfield when the last name pops out of the register. They won't be able to catch us then."

"I don't like it," said George. "It will be the first time I ever walked out on a job. Besides, it would make them suspicious. No, I'll sit tight and take what comes."

"I *still* don't like it," he said, seven days later, as the tough little mountain ponies carried them down the winding road. "And don't you think I'm running away because I'm afraid. I'm just sorry for those poor old guys up there, and I don't want to be around when they find what suckers they've been. Wonder how Sam will take it?"

"It's funny," replied Chuck, "but when I said good-by I got the idea he knew we were walking out on him—and that he didn't care because he knew the machine was running smoothly and that the job would soon be finished. After that—well, of course, for him there just isn't any After That. . . ."

George turned in his saddle and stared back up the mountain road. This was the last place from which one could get a clear view of the lamasery. The squat, angular buildings were silhouetted against the afterglow of the sunset: here and there, lights gleamed like portholes in the side of an ocean liner. Electric lights, of course, sharing the same circuit as the Mark V. How much longer would they share it? wondered George. Would the monks smash up the computer in their rage and disappointment? Or would they just sit down quietly and begin their calculations all over again?

He knew exactly what was happening up on the mountain at this very moment. The high lama and his assistants would be sitting in their silk robes, inspecting the sheets as the junior monks carried them away from the typewriters and pasted them into the great volumes. No one would be saying anything. The only sound would be the incessant patter, the never-ending rainstorm of the keys hitting the paper, for the Mark V itself was utterly silent as it flashed through its thousands of calculations a second. Three months of this, thought George, was enough to start anyone climbing up the wall.

"There she is!" called Chuck, pointing down into the valley. "Ain't she beautiful!"

She certainly was, thought George. The battered old DC3 lay at the end of the runway like a tiny silver cross. In two hours she would be bearing them away to freedom and sanity. It was a thought worth savoring like a fine liqueur. George let it roll round his mind as the pony trudged patiently down the slope.

The swift night of the high Himalayas was now almost upon them. Fortunately, the road was very good, as roads went in that region, and they were both carrying torches. There was not the slightest danger, only a certain discomfort from the bitter cold. The sky overhead was perfectly clear, and ablaze with the familiar, friendly stars. At least there would be no risk, thought George, of the pilot being unable to take off because of weather conditions. That had been his only remaining worry.

He began to sing, but gave it up after a while. This vast arena of mountains, gleaming like whitely hooded ghosts on every side, did not encourage such ebullience. Presently George glanced at his watch.

"Should be there in an hour," he called back over his shoulder to Chuck. Then he added, in an afterthought: "Wonder if the computer's finished its run. It was due about now."

Chuck didn't reply, so George swung round in his saddle. He could just see Chuck's face, a white oval turned toward the sky.

"Look," whispered Chuck, and George lifted his eyes to heaven. (There is always a last time for everything.)

Overhead, without any fuss, the stars were going out.

## REFUGEE

"WHEN HE comes aboard," said Captain Saunders, as he waited for the landing ramp to extrude itself, "what the devil shall I call him?"

There was a thoughtful silence while the navigation officer and the assistant pilot considered this problem in etiquette. Then Mitchell locked the main control panel, and the ship's multitudinous mechanisms lapsed into unconsciousness as power was withdrawn from them.

"The correct address," he drawled slowly, "is 'Your Royal Highness.' "

"Huh!" snorted the captain. "I'll be damned if I'll call anyone *that*!"

"In these progressive days," put in Chambers helpfully, "I believe that 'Sir' is quite sufficient. But there's no need to worry if you forget: it's been a long time since anyone went to the Tower. Besides, this Henry isn't as tough a proposition as the one who had all the wives."

"From all accounts," added Mitchell, "he's a very pleasant young man. Quite intelligent, too. He's often been known to ask people technical questions that they couldn't answer."

Captain Saunders ignored the implications of this remark, beyond resolving that if Prince Henry wanted to know how a Field Compensation Drive Generator worked, then Mitchell could do the explaining. He got gingerly to his feet—they'd been operating on half a gravity during flight, and now they were on Earth, he felt like a ton of bricks—and started to make his way along the corridors that led to the lower air lock. With an oily purring, the great curving door side-stepped out of his way. Adjusting his smile, he walked out to meet the television cameras and the heir to the British throne.

The man who would, presumably, one day be Henry IX

of England was still in his early twenties. He was slightly
below average height, and had fine-drawn, regular features that
really lived up to all the genealogical clichés. Captain Saunders,
who came from Dallas and had no intention of being impressed by any prince, found himself unexpectedly moved by
the wide, sad eyes. They were eyes that had seen too many
receptions and parades, that had had to watch countless totally
uninteresting things, that had never been allowed to stray far
from the carefully planned official routes. Looking at that
proud but weary face, Captain Saunders glimpsed for the first
time the ultimate loneliness of royalty. All his dislike of that
institution became suddenly trivial against its real defect:
what was wrong with the Crown was the unfairness of
inflicting such a burden on any human being. . . .

The passageways of the *Centaurus* were too narrow to
allow for general sight-seeing, and it was soon clear that it
suited Prince Henry very well to leave his entourage behind.
Once they had begun moving through the ship, Saunders lost
all his stiffness and reserve, and within a few minutes was
treating the prince exactly like any other visitor. He did not
realize that one of the earliest lessons royalty has to learn is
that of putting people at their ease.

"You know, Captain," said the prince wistfully, "this is a
big day for us. I've always hoped that one day it would be
possible for spaceships to operate from England. But it still
seems strange to have a port of our own here, after all these
years. Tell me—did you ever have much to do with rockets?"

"Well, I had some training on them, but they were already
on the way out before I graduated. I was lucky: some older
men had to go back to school and start all over again—or else
abandon space completely if they couldn't convert to the new
ships."

"It made as much difference as that?"

"Oh yes—when the rocket went, it was as big as the
change from sail to steam. That's an analogy you'll often
hear, by the way. There was a glamour about the old rockets,
just as there was about the old windjammers, which these
modern ships haven't got. When the *Centaurus* takes off, she
goes up as quietly as a balloon—and as slowly, if she wants
to. But a rocket blast-off shook the ground for miles, and
you'd be deaf for days if you were too near the launching
apron. Still, you'll know all that from the old news recordings."

The prince smiled.

"Yes," he said. "I've often run through them at the Palace.
I think I've watched every incident in all the pioneering

expeditions. I was sorry to see the end of the rockets, too. But we could never have had a spaceport here on Salisbury Plain—the vibration would have shaken down Stonehenge!"

"Stonehenge?" queried Saunders as he held open a hatch and let the prince through into Hold Number 3.

"Ancient monument—one of the most famous stone circles in the world. It's really impressive, and about three thousand years old. See it if you can—it's only ten miles from here."

Captain Sauders had some difficulty in suppressing a smile. What an odd country this was: where else, he wondered, would you find contrasts like this? It made him feel very young and raw when he remembered that back home Billy the Kid was ancient history, and there was hardly anything in the whole of Texas as much as five hundred years old. For the first time he began to realize what tradition meant: it gave Prince Henry something that he could never possess. Poise—self-confidence, yes, that was it. And a pride that was somehow free from arrogance because it took itself so much for granted that it never had to be asserted.

It was surprising how many questions Prince Henry managed to ask in the thirty minutes that had been allotted for his tour of the freighter. They were not the routine questions that people asked out of politeness, quite uninterested in the answers. H.R.H. Prince Henry knew a lot about spaceships, and Captain Saunders felt completely exhausted when he handed his distinguished guest back to the reception committee, which had been waiting outside the *Centaurus* with well-simulated patience.

"Thank you very much, Captain," said the prince as they shook hands in the air lock. "I've not enjoyed myself so much for ages. I hope you have a pleasant stay in England, and a successful voyage." Then his retinue whisked him away, and the port officials, frustrated until now, came aboard to check the ship's papers.

"Well," said Mitchell when it was all over, "what did you think of our Prince of Wales?"

"He surprised me," answered Saunders frankly. "I'd never have guessed he was a prince. I always thought they were rather dumb. But heck, he *knew* the principles of the Field Drive! Has he ever been up in space?"

"Once, I think. Just a hop above the atmosphere in a Space Force ship. It didn't even reach orbit before it came back again—but the Prime Minister nearly had a fit. There were questions in the House and editorials in the *Times*. Everyone decided that the heir to the throne was too valuable to risk in these newfangled inventions. So, though he has the rank of commodore in the Royal Space Force, he's never even been to the moon."

"The poor guy," said Captain Saunders.

He had three days to burn, since it was not the captain's job to supervise the loading of the ship or the preflight maintenance. Saunders knew skippers who hung around breathing heavily on the necks of the servicing engineers, but he wasn't that type. Besides, he wanted to see London. He had been to Mars and Venus and the moon, but this was his first visit to England. Mitchell and Chambers filled him with useful information and put him on the monorail to London before dashing off to see their own families. They would be returning to the spaceport a day before he did, to see that everything was in order. It was a great relief having officers one could rely on so implicitly: they were unimaginative and cautious, but thoroughgoing almost to a fault. If *they* said that everything was shipshape, Saunders knew he could take off without qualms.

The sleek, streamlined cylinder whistled across the carefully tailored landscape. It was so close to the ground, and traveling so swiftly, that one could only gather fleeting impressions of the towns and fields that flashed by. Everything, thought Saunders, was so incredibly compact, and on such a Lilliputian scale. There were no open spaces, no fields more than a mile long in any direction. It was enough to give a Texan claustrophobia—particularly a Texan who also happened to be a space pilot.

The sharply defined edge of London appeared like the bulwark of some walled city on the horizon. With few exceptions, the buildings were quite low—perhaps fifteen or twenty stories in height. The monorail shot through a narrow canyon, over a very attractive park, across a river that was presumably the Thames, and then came to rest with a steady, powerful surge of deceleration. A loud-speaker announced, in a modest voice that seemed afraid of being overheard: "This is Paddington. Passengers for the North please remain seated." Saunders pulled his baggage down from the rack and headed out into the station.

As he made for the entrance to the Underground, he passed a bookstall and glanced at the magazines on display. About half of them, it seemed, carried photographs of Prince Henry or other members of the royal family. This, thought Saunders, was altogether too much of a good thing. He also noticed that all the evening papers showed the prince entering or leaving the *Centaurus,* and bought copies to read in the subway—he begged its pardon, the "Tube."

The editorial comments had a monotonous similarity. At last, they rejoiced, England need no longer take a back seat among the space-going nations. Now it was possible to operate a space fleet without having a million square miles of desert: the silent, gravity-defying ships of today could land, if need be, in Hyde Park, without even disturbing the ducks on the Serpentine. Saunders found it odd that this sort of patriotism had managed to survive into the age of space, but he guessed that the British had felt it pretty badly when they'd had to borrow launching sites from the Australians, the Americans, and the Russians.

The London Underground was still, after a century and a half, the best transport system in the world, and it deposited Saunders safely at his destination less than ten minutes after he had left Paddington. In ten minutes the *Centaurus* could have covered fifty thousand miles; but space, after all, was not quite so crowded as this. Nor were the orbits of space craft so tortuous as the streets Saunders had to negotiate to reach his hotel. All attempts to straighten out London had failed dismally, and it was fifteen minutes before he completed the last hundred yards of his journey.

He stripped off his jacket and collapsed thankfully on his bed. Three quiet, carefree days all to himself: it seemed too good to be true.

It was. He had barely taken a deep breath when the phone rang.

"Captain Saunders? I'm so glad we found you. This is the B.B.C. We have a program called 'In Town Tonight' and we were wondering . . ."

The thud of the air-lock door was the sweetest sound Saunders had heard for days. Now he was safe; nobody could get at him here in his armored fortress, which would soon be far out in the freedom of space. It was not that he had been treated badly: on the contrary, he had been treated altogether too well. He had made four (or was it five?) appearances on various TV programs; he had been to more parties than he could remember; he had acquired several hundred new friends and (the way his head felt now) forgotten all his old ones.

"Who started the rumor," he said to Mitchell as they met at the port, "that the British were reserved and stand-offish? Heaven help me if I ever meet a *demonstrative* Englishman."

"I take it," replied Mitchell, "that you had a good time."

"Ask me tomorrow," Saunders replied. "I may have re-integrated my psyche by then."

"I saw you on that quiz program last night," remarked Chambers. "You looked pretty ghastly."

"Thank you: that's just the sort of sympathetic encouragement I need at the moment. I'd like to see you think of a synonym for 'jejune' after you'd been up until three in the morning."

"Vapid," replied Chambers promptly.

"Insipid," said Mitchell, not to be outdone.

"You win. Let's have those overhaul schedules and see what the engineers have been up to."

Once seated at the control desk, Captain Saunders quickly became his usual efficient self. He was home again, and his training took over. He knew exactly what to do, and would do it with automatic precision. To right and left of him, Mitchell and Chambers were checking their instruments and calling the control tower.

It took them an hour to carry out the elaborate preflight routine. When the last signature had been attached to the last sheet of instructions, and the last red light on the monitor panel had turned to green, Saunders flopped back in his seat and lit a cigarette. They had ten minutes to spare before take-off.

"One day," he said, "I'm going to come to England incognito to find what makes the place tick. I don't understand how you can crowd so many people onto one little island without it sinking."

"Huh," snorted Chambers. "You should see Holland. That makes England look as wide open as Texas."

"And then there's this royal family business. Do you know, wherever I went everybody kept asking me how I got on with Prince Henry—what we'd talked about—didn't I think he was a fine guy, and so on. Frankly, I got fed up with it. I can't imagine how you've managed to stand it for a thousand years."

"Don't think that the royal family's been popular all the time," replied Mitchell. "Remember what happened to Charles the First? And some of the things we said about the early Georges were quite as rude as the remarks your people made later."

"We just happen to like tradition," said Chambers. "We're not afraid to change when the time comes, but as far as the royal family is concerned—well, it's unique and we're rather fond of it. Just the way you feel about the Statue of Liberty."

"Not a fair example. I don't think it's right to put human beings up on a pedestal and treat them as if they're—well, minor deities. Look at Prince Henry, for instance. Do you think he'll ever have a chance of doing the things he really wants to do? I saw him three times on TV when I was in London. The first time he was opening a new school somewhere; then he was giving a speech to the Worshipful Company of Fishmongers at the Guildhall (I swear I'm not making *that* up), and finally he was receiving an address of welcome from the mayor of Podunk, or whatever your equivalent is." ("Wigan," interjected Mitchell.) "I think I'd rather be in jail than live that sort of life. Why can't you leave the poor guy alone?"

For once, neither Mitchell nor Chambers rose to the challenge. Indeed, they maintained a somewhat frigid silence. That's torn it, thought Saunders. I should have kept my big mouth shut; now I've hurt their feelings. I should have remembered that advice I read somewhere: "The British have two religions—cricket and the royal family. Never attempt to criticize either."

The awkward pause was broken by the radio and the voice of the spaceport controller.

"Control to *Centaurus*. Your flight lane clear. O.K. to lift."

"Take-off program starting—*now!*" replied Saunders, throwing the master switch. Then he leaned back, his eyes taking in the entire control panel, his hands clear of the board but ready for instant action.

He was tense but completely confident. Better brains than his—brains of metal and crystal and flashing electron streams —were in charge of the *Centaurus* now. If necessary, he could take command, but he had never yet lifted a ship manually and never expected to do so. If the automatics failed, he would cancel the take-off and sit here on Earth until the fault had been cleared up.

The main field went on, and weight ebbed from the *Centaurus*. There were protesting groans from the ship's hull and structure as the strains redistributed themselves. The curved arms of the landing cradle were carrying no load now; the slightest breath of wind would carry the freighter away into the sky.

Control called from the tower: "Your weight now zero: check calibration."

Saunders looked at his meters. The upthrust of the field would now exactly equal the weight of the ship, and the meter readings should agree with the totals on the loading schedules. In at least one instance this check had revealed the presence of a stowaway on board a spaceship—the gauges were as sensitive as that.

"One million, five hundred and sixty thousand, four hundred and twenty kilograms," Saunders read off from the thrust indicators. "Pretty good—it checks to within fifteen kilos. The first time I've been underweight, though. You could have taken on some more candy for that plump girl friend of yours in Port Lowell, Mitch."

The assistant pilot gave a rather sickly grin. He had never quite lived down a blind date on Mars which had given him a completely unwarranted reputation for preferring statuesque blondes.

There was no sense of motion, but the *Centaurus* was now falling up into the summer sky as her weight was not only neutralized but reversed. To the watchers below, she would be a swiftly mounting star, a silver globule climbing through and beyond the clouds. Around her, the blue of the atmosphere was deepening into the eternal darkness of space. Like a bead moving along an invisible wire, the freighter was following the pattern of radio waves that would lead her from world to world.

This, thought Captain Saunders, was his twenty-sixth take-off from Earth. But the wonder would never die, nor would he ever outgrow the feeling of power it gave him to sit here at the control panel, the master of forces beyond even the dreams of mankind's ancient gods. No two departures were ever the same; some were into the dawn, some toward the sunset, some above a cloud-veiled Earth, some through clear and sparkling skies. Space itself might be unchanging, but on Earth the same pattern never recurred, and no man ever looked twice at the same landscape or the same sky. Down there the Atlantic waves were marching eternally toward Europe, and high above them—but so far below the *Centaurus!* —the glittering bands of cloud were advancing before the same winds. England began to merge into the continent, and the European coast line became foreshortened and misty as it sank hull down beyond the curve of the world. At the frontier of the west, a fugitive stain on the horizon was the first hint of America. With a single glance, Captain Saunders could span all the leagues across which Columbus had labored half a thousand years ago.

With the silence of limitless power, the ship shook itself free from the last bonds of Earth. To an outside observer, the only sign of the energies it was expending would have been the dull red glow from the radiation fins around the vessel's equator, as the heat loss from the mass-converters was dissipated into space.

"14:03:45," wrote Captain Saunders neatly in the log. "Escape velocity attained. Course deviation negligible."

There was little point in making the entry. The modest 25,000 miles an hour that had been the almost unattainable goal of the first astronauts had no practical significance now, since the *Centaurus* was still accelerating and would continue to gain speed for hours. But it had a profound psychological meaning. Until this moment, if power had failed, they would have fallen back to Earth. But now gravity could never recapture them: they had achieved the freedom of space, and could take their pick of the planets. In practice, of course, there would be several kinds of hell to pay if they did not pick Mars and deliver their cargo according to plan. But Captain Saunders, like all spacemen, was fundamentally a romantic. Even on a milk run like this he would sometimes dream of the ringed glory of Saturn or the somber Neptunian wastes, lit by the distant fires of the shrunken sun.

An hour after take-off, according to the hallowed ritual, Chambers left the course computer to its own devices and produced the three glasses that lived beneath the chart table. As he drank the traditional toast to Newton, Oberth, and Einstein, Saunders wondered how this little ceremony had originated. Space crews had certainly been doing it for at least sixty years: perhaps it could be traced back to the legendary rocket engineer who made the remark, "I've burned more alcohol in sixty seconds than you've ever sold across this lousy bar."

Two hours later, the last course correction that the tracking stations on Earth could give them had been fed into the computer. From now on, until Mars came sweeping up ahead, they were on their own. It was a lonely thought, yet a curiously exhilarating one. Saunders savored it in his mind. There were just the three of them here—and no one else within a million miles.

In the circumstances, the detonation of an atomic bomb could hardly have been more shattering than the modest knock on the cabin door. . . .

Captain Saunders had never been so startled in his life. With a yelp that had already left him before he had a chance to suppress it, he shot out of his seat and rose a full yard before the ship's residual gravity field dragged him back. Chambers and Mitchell, on the other hand, behaved with traditional British phlegm. They swiveled in their bucket seats, stared at the door, and then waited for their captain to take action.

It took Saunders several seconds to recover. Had he been confronted with what might be called a normal emergency, he would already have been halfway into a space suit. But a diffident knock on the door of the control cabin, when everybody else in the ship was sitting beside him, was not a fair test.

A stowaway was simply impossible. The danger had been so obvious, right from the beginning of commercial space flight, that the most stringent precautions had been taken against it. One of his officers, Saunders knew, would always have been on duty during loading; no one could possibly have crept in unobserved. Then there had been the detailed preflight inspection, carried out by both Mitchell and Chambers. Finally, there was the weight check at the moment before take-off; *that* was conclusive. No, a stowaway was totally . . .

The knock on the door sounded again. Captain Saunders clenched his fists and squared his jaw. In a few minutes, he thought, some romantic idiot was going to be very, very sorry.

"Open the door, Mr. Mitchell," Saunders growled. In a single long stride, the assistant pilot crossed the cabin and jerked open the hatch.

For an age, it seemed, no one spoke. Then the stowaway, wavering slightly in the low gravity, came into the cabin. He was completely self-possessed, and looked very pleased with himself.

"Good afternoon, Captain Saunders," he said, "I must apologize for this sudden intrusion."

Saunders swallowed hard. Then, as the pieces of the jigsaw fell into place, he looked first at Mitchell, then at Chambers. Both of his officers stared guilelessly back at him with expressions of ineffable innocence. "So *that's* it," he said bitterly. There was no need for any explanations: everything was perfectly clear. It was easy to picture the complicated negotiations, the midnight meetings, the falsification of records, the off-loading of nonessential cargoes that his trusted colleagues had been conducting behind his back. He was sure it was a most interesting story, but he didn't want to hear about it now. He was too busy wondering what the *Manual of Space Law* would have to say about a situation like this, though he was already gloomily certain that it would be of no use to him at all.

It was too late to turn back, of course: the conspirators wouldn't have made an elementary miscalculation like that.

He would just have to make the best of what looked to be the trickiest voyage in his career.

He was still trying to think of something to say when the PRIORITY signal started flashing on the radio board. The stowaway looked at his watch.

"I was expecting that," he said. "It's probably the Prime Minister. I think I'd better speak to the poor man."

Saunders thought so too.

"Very well, Your Royal Highness," he said sulkily, and with such emphasis that the title sounded almost like an insult. Then, feeling much put upon, he retired into a corner.

It was the Prime Minister all right, and he sounded very upset. Several times he used the phrase "your duty to your people" and once there was a distinct catch in his throat as he said something about "devotion of your subjects to the Crown." Saunders realized, with some surprise, that he really meant it.

While this emotional harangue was in progress, Mitchell leaned over to Saunders and whispered in his ear:

"The old boy's on a sticky wicket, and he knows it. The people will be behind the prince when they hear what's happened. Everybody knows he's been trying to get into space for years."

"I wish he hadn't chosen *my* ship," said Saunders. "And I'm not sure that this doesn't count as mutiny."

"The heck it does. Mark my words—when this is all over you'll be the only Texan to have the Order of the Garter. Won't that be nice for you?"

"Shush!" said Chambers. The prince was speaking, his words winging back across the abyss that now sundered him from the island he would one day rule.

"I am sorry, Mr. Prime Minister," he said, "if I've caused you any alarm. I will return as soon as it is convenient. Someone has to do everything for the first time, and I felt the moment had come for a member of my family to leave Earth. It will be a valuable part of my education, and will make me more fitted to carry out my duty. Good-by."

He dropped the microphone and walked over to the observation window—the only spaceward-looking port on the entire ship. Saunders watched him standing there, proud and lonely—but contented now. And as he saw the prince staring out at the stars which he had at last attained, all his annoyance and indignation slowly evaporated.

No one spoke for a long time. Then Prince Henry tore his gaze away from the blinding splendor beyond the port, looked at Captain Saunders, and smiled.

"Where's the galley, Captain?" he asked. "I may be out of practice, but when I used to go scouting I was the best cook in my patrol."

Saunders slowly relaxed, then smiled back. The tension seemed to lift from the control room. Mars was still a long way off, but he knew now that this wasn't going to be such a bad trip after all. . . .

# THE OTHER SIDE OF THE SKY

### *Special Delivery*

I CAN still remember the excitement, back in 1957, when Russia launched the first artificial satellites and managed to hang a few pounds of instruments up here above the atmosphere. Of course, I was only a kid at the time, but I went out in the evening like everyone else, trying to spot those little magnesium spheres as they zipped through the twilight sky hundreds of miles above my head. It's strange to think that some of them are still there—but that now they're *below* me, and I'd have to look down toward Earth if I wanted to see them. . . .

Yes, a lot has happened in the last forty years, and sometimes I'm afraid that you people down on Earth take the space stations for granted, forgetting the skill and science and courage that went to make them. How often do you stop to think that all your long-distance phone calls, and most of your TV programs, are routed through one or the other of the satellites? And how often do you give any credit to the meteorologists up here for the fact that weather forecasts are no longer the joke they were to our grandfathers, but are dead accurate ninety-nine per cent of the time?

It was a rugged life, back in the seventies, when I went up to work on the outer stations. They were being rushed into operation to open up the millions of new TV and radio circuits which would be available as soon as we had transmitters out in space that could beam programs to anywhere on the globe.

The first artificial satellites had been very close to Earth, but the three stations forming the great triangle of the Relay

Chain had to be twenty-two thousand miles up, spaced equally around the equator. At this altitude—and at no other—they would take exactly a day to go around their orbit, and so would stay poised forever over the same spot on the turning Earth.

In my time I've worked on all three of the stations, but my first tour of duty was aboard Relay Two. That's almost exactly over Entebbe, Uganda, and provides service for Europe, Africa, and most of Asia. Today it's a huge structure hundreds of yards across, beaming thousands of simultaneous programs down to the hemisphere beneath it as it carries the radio traffic of half the world. But when I saw it for the first time from the port of the ferry rocket that carried me up to orbit, it looked like a junk pile adrift in space. Prefabricated parts were floating around in hopeless confusion, and it seemed impossible that any order could ever emerge from this chaos.

Accommodation for the technical staff and assembling crews was primitive, consisting of a few unserviceable ferry rockets that had been stripped of everything except air purifiers. "The Hulks," we christened them; each man had just enough room for himself and a couple of cubic feet of personal belongings. There was a fine irony in the fact that we were living in the midst of infinite space—and hadn't room to swing a cat.

It was a great day when we heard that the first pressurized living quarters were on their way up to us—complete with needle-jet shower baths that would operate even here, where water—like everything else—had no weight. Unless you've lived aboard an overcrowded spaceship, you won't appreciate what that meant. We could throw away our damp sponges and feel really clean at last. . . .

Nor were the showers the only luxury promised us. On the way up from Earth was an inflatable lounge spacious enough to hold no fewer than eight people, a microfilm library, a magnetic billiard table, lightweight chess sets, and similar novelties for bored spacemen. The very thought of all these comforts made our cramped life in the Hulks seem quite unendurable, even though we were being paid about a thousand dollars a week to endure it.

Starting from the Second Refueling Zone, two thousand miles above Earth, the eagerly awaited ferry rocket would take about six hours to climb up to us with its precious cargo. I was off duty at the time, and stationed myself at the telescope where I'd spent most of my scanty leisure. It was impossible to grow tired of exploring the great world hanging there in space beside us; with the highest power of the telescope, one seemed to be only a few miles above the surface. When there were no clouds and the seeing was good, objects the size of a small house were easily visible. I had never been to Africa, but I grew to know it well while I was off duty in Station Two. You may not believe this, but I've often spotted elephants moving across the plains, and the immense herds of zebras and antelopes were easy to see as they flowed back and forth like living tides on the great reservations.

But my favorite spectacle was the dawn coming up over the mountains in the heart of the continent. The line of sunlight would come sweeping across the Indian Ocean, and the new day would extinguish the tiny, twinkling galaxies of the cities shining in the darkness below me. Long before the sun had reached the lowlands around them, the peaks of Kilimanjaro and Mount Kenya would be blazing in the dawn, brilliant stars still surrounded by the night. As the sun rose higher, the day would march swiftly down their slopes and the valleys would fill with light. Earth would then be at its first quarter, waxing toward full.

Twelve hours later, I would see the reverse process as the same mountains caught the last rays of the setting sun. They would blaze for a little while in the narrow belt of twilight; then Earth would spin into darkness, and night would fall upon Africa.

It was not the beauty of the terrestrial globe I was concerned with now. Indeed, I was not even looking at Earth, but at the fierce blue-white star high above the western edge of the planet's disk. The automatic freighter was eclipsed in Earth's shadow; what I was seeing was the incandescent flare of its rockets as they drove it up on its twenty-thousand-mile climb.

I had watched ships ascending to us so often that I knew every stage of their maneuver by heart. So when the rockets didn't wink out, but continued to burn steadily, I knew within seconds that something was wrong. In sick, helpless fury I watched all our longed-for comforts—and, worse still, our mail!—moving faster and faster along the unintended orbit. The freighter's autopilot had jammed; had there been a human pilot aboard, he could have overridden the controls and cut the motor, but now all the fuel that should have driven the ferry on its two-way trip was being burned in one continuous blast of power.

By the time the fuel tanks had emptied, and that distant star had flickered and died in the field of my telescope, the tracking stations had confirmed what I already knew. The freighter was moving far too fast for Earth's gravity to recapture it—indeed, it was heading into the cosmic wilderness beyond Pluto. . . .

It took a long time for morale to recover, and it only made matters worse when someone in the computing section worked out the future history of our errant freighter. You see, nothing is ever really lost in space. Once you've calculated its orbit, you know where it is until the end of eternity. As we watched our lounge, our library, our games, our mail receding to the far horizons of the solar system, we knew that it would all come back one day in perfect condition. If we have a ship standing by it will be easy to intercept it the second time it comes around the sun—quite early in the spring of the year A.D. 15,862.

## Feathered Friend

To THE best of my knowledge, there's never been a regulation that forbids one to keep pets in a space station. No one ever thought it was necessary—and even had such a rule existed, I am quite certain that Sven Olsen would have ignored it.

With a name like that, you will picture Sven at once as a six-foot-six Nordic giant, built like a bull and with a voice to match. Had this been so, his chances of getting a job in space would have been very slim; actually he was a wiry little fellow, like most of the early spacers, and managed to qualify easily for the 150-pound bonus that kept so many of us on a reducing diet.

Sven was one of our best construction men, and excelled at the tricky and specialized work of collecting assorted girders as they floated around in free fall, making them do the slow-motion, three-dimensional ballet that would get them into their right positions, and fusing the pieces together when they were precisely dovetailed into the intended pattern. I never tired of watching him and his gang as the station grew under their hands like a giant jigsaw puzzle; it was a skilled and difficult job, for a space suit is not the most convenient of garbs in which to work. However, Sven's team had one great advantage over the construction gangs you see putting up skyscrapers down on Earth. They could step back and admire their handiwork without being abruptly parted from it by gravity. . . .

Don't ask me why Sven wanted a pet, or why he chose the one he did. I'm not a psychologist, but I must admit that his selection was very sensible. Claribel weighed practically nothing, her food requirements were infinitesimal—and she was not worried, as most animals would have been, by the absence of gravity.

I first became aware that Claribel was aboard when I was sitting in the little cubbyhole laughingly called my office, checking through my lists of technical stores to decide what items we'd be running out of next. When I heard the musical whistle beside my ear, I assumed that it had come over the station intercom, and waited for an announcement to follow. It didn't; instead, there was a long and involved pattern of melody that made me look up with such a start that I forgot all about the angle beam just behind my head. When the stars had ceased to explode before my eyes, I had my first view of Claribel.

She was a small yellow canary, hanging in the air as motionless as a hummingbird—and with much less effort, for her wings were quietly folded along her sides. We stared at each other for a minute; then, before I had quite recovered my wits, she did a curious kind of backward loop I'm sure no earthbound canary had ever managed, and departed with a few leisurely flicks. It was quite obvious that she'd already learned how to operate in the absence of gravity, and did not believe in doing unnecessary work.

Sven didn't confess to her ownership for several days, and by that time it no longer mattered, because Claribel was a general pet. He had smuggled her up on the last ferry from Earth, when he came back from leave—partly, he claimed, out of sheer scientific curiosity. He wanted to see just how a bird would operate when it had no weight but could still use its wings.

Claribel thrived and grew fat. On the whole, we had little trouble concealing our unauthorized guest when VIP's from Earth came visiting. A space station has more hiding places than you can count; the only problem was that Claribel got rather noisy when she was upset, and we sometimes had to think fast to explain the curious peeps and whistles that came from ventilating shafts and storage bulkheads. There were a couple of narrow escapes—but then who would dream of looking for a canary in a space station?

We were now on twelve-hour watches, which was not as bad as it sounds, since you need little sleep in space. Though of course there is no "day" and "night" when you are floating in permanent sunlight, it was still convenient to stick to the terms. Certainly when I woke up that "morning" it felt like 6:00 A.M. on Earth. I had a nagging headache, and

vague memories of fitful, disturbed dreams. It took me ages
to undo my bunk straps, and I was still only half awake
when I joined the remainder of the duty crew in the mess.
Breakfast was unusually quiet, and there was one seat vacant.

"Where's Sven?" I asked, not very much caring.

"He's looking for Claribel," someone answered. "Says he
can't find her anywhere. She usually wakes him up."

Before I could retort that she usually woke me up, too,
Sven came in through the doorway, and we could see at once
that something was wrong. He slowly opened his hand, and
there lay a tiny bundle of yellow feathers, with two clenched
claws sticking pathetically up into the air.

"What happened?" we asked, all equally distressed.

"I don't know," said Sven mournfully. "I just found her
like this."

"Let's have a look at her," said Jock Duncan, our cook-
doctor-dietitian. We all waited in hushed silence while he
held Claribel against his ear in an attempt to detect any
heartbeat.

Presently he shook his head. "I can't hear anything, but
that doesn't prove she's dead. I've never listened to a canary's
heart," he added rather apologetically.

"Give her a shot of oxygen," suggested somebody, pointing
to the green-banded emergency cylinder in its recess beside
the door. Everyone agreed that this was an excellent idea,
and Claribel was tucked snugly into a face mask that was
large enough to serve as a complete oxygen tent for her.

To our delighted surprise, she revived at once. Beaming
broadly, Sven removed the mask, and she hopped onto his
fingers. She gave her series of "Come to the cookhouse, boys"
trills—then promptly keeled over again.

"I don't get it," lamented Sven. "What's wrong with her?
She's never done this before."

For the last few minutes, something had been tugging at
my memory. My mind seemed to be very sluggish that
morning, as if I was still unable to cast off the burden of
sleep. I felt that I could do with some of that oxygen—but
before I could reach the mask, understanding exploded in
my brain. I whirled on the duty engineer and said urgently:

"Jim! There's something wrong with the air! That's why
Claribel's passed out. I've just remembered that miners used
to carry canaries down to warn them of gas."

"Nonsense!" said Jim. "The alarms would have gone off.
We've got duplicate circuits, operating independently."

"Er—the second alarm circuit isn't connected up yet," his
assistant reminded him. That shook Jim; he left without a

word, while we stood arguing and passing the oxygen bottle around like a pipe of peace.

He came back ten minutes later with a sheepish expression. It was one of those accidents that couldn't possibly happen; we'd had one of our rare eclipses by Earth's shadow that night; part of the air purifier had frozen up, and the single alarm in the circuit had failed to go off. Half a million dollars' worth of chemical and electronic engineering had let us down completely. Without Claribel, we should soon have been slightly dead.

So now, if you visit any space station, don't be surprised if you hear an inexplicable snatch of bird song. There's no need to be alarmed: on the contrary, in fact. It will mean that you're being doubly safeguarded, at practically no extra expense.

## Take a Deep Breath

A LONG TIME AGO I discovered that people who've never left Earth have certain fixed ideas about conditions in space. Everyone "knows," for example, that a man dies instantly and horribly when exposed to the vacuum that exists beyond the atmosphere. You'll find numerous gory descriptions of exploded space travelers in the popular literature, and I won't spoil your appetite by repeating them here. Many of those tales, indeed, are basically true. I've pulled men back through the air lock who were very poor advertisements for space flight.

Yet, at the same time, there are exceptions to every rule —even this one. I should know, for I learned the hard way.

We were on the last stages of building Communications Satellite Two; all the main units had been joined together, the living quarters had been pressurized, and the station had been given the slow spin around its axis that had restored the unfamiliar sensation of weight. I say "slow," but at its rim our two-hundred-foot-diameter wheel was turning at thirty miles an hour. We had, of course, no sense of motion, but the centrifugal force caused by this spin gave us about half the weight we would have possessed on Earth. That was enough to stop things from drifting around, yet not enough to make us feel uncomfortably sluggish after our weeks with no weight at all.

Four of us were sleeping in the small cylindrical cabin known as Bunkhouse Number 6 on the night that it happened. The bunkhouse was at the very rim of the station; if you imagine a bicycle wheel, with a string of sausages replacing the tire, you have a good idea of the layout. Bunkhouse Number 6 was one of these sausages, and we were slumbering peacefully inside it.

I was awakened by a sudden jolt that was not violent enough to cause me alarm, but which did make me sit up and wonder what had happened. Anything unusual in a space station demands instant attention, so I reached for the intercom switch by my bed. "Hello, Central," I called. "What was that?"

There was no reply; the line was dead.

Now thoroughly alarmed, I jumped out of bed—and had an even bigger shock. *There was no gravity.* I shot up to the ceiling before I was able to grab a stanchion and bring myself to a halt, at the cost of a sprained wrist.

It was impossible for the entire station to have suddenly stopped rotating. There was only one answer; the failure of the intercom and, as I quickly discovered, of the lighting circuit as well forced us to face the appalling truth. We were no longer part of the station; our little cabin had somehow come adrift, and had been slung off into space like a raindrop falling off a spinning flywheel.

There were no windows through which we could look out, but we were not in complete darkness, for the battery-powered emergency lights had come on. All the main air vents had closed automatically when the pressure dropped. For the time being, we could live in our own private atmosphere, even though it was not being renewed. Unfortunately, a steady whistling told us that the air we did have was escaping through a leak somewhere in the cabin.

There was no way of telling what had happened to the rest of the station. For all we knew, the whole structure might have come to pieces, and all our colleagues might be dead or in the same predicament as we—drifting through space in leaking cans of air. Our one slim hope was the possibility that we were the only castaways, that the rest of the station was intact and had been able to send a rescue team to find us. After all, we were receding at no more than thirty miles an hour, and one of the rocket scooters could catch up to us in minutes.

It actually took an hour, though without the evidence of my watch I should never have believed that it was so short a time. We were now gasping for breath—and the gauge on our single emergency oxygen tank had dropped to one division above zero.

The banging on the wall seemed like a signal from another world. We banged back vigorously, and a moment later a muffled voice called to us through the wall. Someone outside was lying with his space-suit helmet pressed against the metal, and his shouted words were reaching us by direct conduction. Not as clear as radio—but it worked.

The oxygen gauge crept slowly down to zero while we had our council of war. We would be dead before we could be towed back to the station; yet the rescue ship was only a few feet away from us, with its air lock already open. Our little problem was to cross that few feet—*without* space suits.

We made our plans carefully, rehearsing our actions in the full knowledge that there could be no repeat performance. Then we each took a deep, final swig of oxygen, flushing out our lungs. When we were all ready, I banged on the wall to give the signal to our friends waiting outside.

There was a series of short, staccato raps as the power tools got to work on the thin hull. We clung tightly to the stanchions, as far away as possible from the point of entry, knowing just what would happen. When it came, it was so sudden that the mind couldn't record the sequence of events. The cabin seemed to explode, and a great wind tugged at me. The last trace of air gushed from my lungs, through my already-opened mouth. And then—utter silence, and the stars shining through the gaping hole that led to life.

Believe me, I didn't stop to analyze my sensations. I think —though I can never be sure that it wasn't imagination— that my eyes were smarting and there was a tingling feeling all over my body. And I felt very cold, perhaps because evaporation was already starting from my skin.

The only thing I can be certain of is that uncanny silence. It is never completely quiet in a space station, for there is always the sound of machinery or air pumps. But this was the absolute silence of the empty void, where there is no trace of air to carry sound.

Almost at once we launched ourselves out through the shattered wall, into the full blast of the sun. I was instantly blinded—but that didn't matter, because the men waiting in space suits grabbed me as soon as I emerged and hustled me into the air lock. And there, sound slowly returned as the air rushed in, and we remembered we could breathe again. The entire rescue, they told us later, had lasted just twenty seconds. . . .

Well, we were the founding members of the Vacuum-Breathers' Club. Since then, at least a dozen other men have done the same thing, in similar emergencies. The record time in space is now two minutes; after that, the blood begins to form bubbles as it boils at body temperature, and those bubbles soon get to the heart.

In my case, there was only one aftereffect. For maybe a quarter of a minute I had been exposed to *real* sunlight, not the feeble stuff that filters down through the atmosphere of Earth. Breathing space didn't hurt me at all—but I got the worst dose of sunburn I've ever had in my life.

## Freedom of Space

NOT MANY of you, I suppose, can imagine the time before the satellite relays gave us our present world communications system. When I was a boy, it was impossible to send TV programs across the ocean, or even to establish reliable radio contact around the curve of the Earth without picking up a fine assortment of crackles and bangs on the way. Yet now we take interference-free circuits for granted, and think nothing of seeing our friends on the other side of the globe as clearly as if we were standing face to face. Indeed, it's a simple fact that without the satellite relays, the whole structure of world commerce and industry would collapse. Unless we were up here on the space stations to bounce their messages around the globe, how do you think any of the world's big business organizations could keep their widely scattered electronic brains in touch with each other?

But all this was still in the future, back in the late seventies, when we were finishing work on the Relay Chain. I've already told you about some of our problems and near disasters; they were serious enough at the time, but in the end we overcame them all. The three stations spaced around Earth were no longer piles of girders, air cylinders, and plastic pressure chambers. Their assembly had been completed, we had moved aboard, and could now work in comfort, unhampered by space suits. And we had gravity again, now that the stations had been set slowly spinning. Not real gravity, of course; but centrifugal force feels exactly the same when you're out in space. It was pleasant being able to pour drinks and to sit down without drifting away on the first air current.

Once the three stations had been built, there was still a year's solid work to be done installing all the radio and TV equipment that would lift the world's communications networks into space. It was a great day when we established the first TV link between England and Australia. The signal was beamed up to us in Relay Two, as we sat above the center of Africa, we flashed it across to Three—poised over New Guinea—and they shot it down to Earth again, clear and clean after its ninety-thousand-mile journey.

These, however, were the engineers' private tests. The official opening of the system would be the biggest event in the history of world communication—an elaborate global telecast, in which every nation would take part. It would be a three-hour show, as for the first time the live TV camera roamed around the world, proclaiming to mankind that the last barrier of distance was down.

The program planning, it was cynically believed, had taken as much effort as the building of the space stations in the first place, and of all the problems the planners had to solve, the most difficult was that of choosing a *compère* or master of ceremonies to introduce the items in the elaborate global show that would be watched by half the human race.

Heaven knows how much conniving, blackmail, and downright character assassination went on behind the scenes. All we knew was that a week before the great day, a nonscheduled rocket came up to orbit with Gregory Wendell aboard. This was quite a surprise, since Gregory wasn't as big a TV personality as, say, Jeffers Jackson in the U.S. or Vince Clifford in Britain. However, it seemed that the big boys had canceled each other out, and Gregg had got the coveted job through one of those compromises so well known to politicians.

Gregg had started his career as a disc jockey on a university radio station in the American Midwest, and had worked his way up through the Hollywood and Manhattan night-club circuits until he had a daily, nation-wide program of his own. Apart from his cynical yet relaxed personality, his biggest asset was his deep velvet voice, for which he could probably thank his Negro blood. Even when you flatly disagreed with what he was saying—even, indeed, when he was tearing you to pieces in an interview—it was still a pleasure to listen to him.

We gave him the grand tour of the space station, and even (strictly against regulations) took him out through the air lock in a space suit. He loved it all, but there were two things he liked in particular. "This air you make," he said, "it beats the stuff we have to breathe down in New York. This is the first time my sinus trouble has gone since I went into TV." He also relished the low gravity; at the station's rim, a man had half his normal, Earth weight—and at the axis he had no weight at all.

However, the novelty of his surroundings didn't distract

Gregg from his job. He spent hours at Communications Central, polishing his script and getting his cues right, and studying the dozens of monitor screens that would be his windows on the world. I came across him once while he was running through his introduction of Queen Elizabeth, who would be speaking from Buckingham Palace at the very end of the program. He was so intent on his rehearsal that he never even noticed I was standing beside him.

Well, that telecast is now part of history. For the first time a billion human beings watched a single program that came "live" from every corner of the Earth, and was a roll call of the world's greatest citizens. Hundreds of cameras on land and sea and air looked inquiringly at the turning globe; and at the end there was that wonderful shot of the Earth through a zoom lens on the space station, making the whole planet recede until it was lost among the stars. . . .

There were a few hitches, of course. One camera on the bed of the Atlantic wasn't ready on cue, and we had to spend some extra time looking at the Taj Mahal. And owing to a switching error Russian subtitles were superimposed on the South American transmissions, while half the U.S.S.R. found itself trying to read Spanish. But this was nothing to what *might* have happened.

Through the entire three hours, introducing the famous and the unknown with equal ease, came the mellow yet never orotund flow of Gregg's voice. He did a magnificent job; the congratulations came pouring up the beam the moment the broadcast finished. But he didn't hear them; he made one short, private call to his agent, and then went to bed.

Next morning, the Earth-bound ferry was waiting to take him back to any job he cared to accept. But it left without Gregg Wendell, now junior station announcer of Relay Two.

"They'll think I'm crazy," he said, beaming happily, "but why should I go back to that rat race down there? I've all the universe to look at, I can breathe smog-free air, the low gravity makes me feel a Hercules, and my three darling ex-wives can't get at me." He kissed his hand to the departing rocket. "So long, Earth," he called. "I'll be back when I start pining for Broadway traffic jams and bleary penthouse dawns. And if I get homesick, I can look at anywhere on the planet just by turning a switch. Why, I'm more in the middle of things here than I could ever be on Earth, yet I can cut myself off from the human race whenever I want to."

He was still smiling as he watched the ferry begin the long fall back to Earth, toward the fame and fortune that could have been his. And then, whistling cheerfully, he left the observation lounge in eight-foot strides to read the weather forecast for Lower Patagonia.

## Passer-by

IT's ONLY fair to warn you, right at the start, that this is a story with no ending. But it has a definite beginning, for it was while we were both students at Astrotech that I met Julie. She was in her final year of solar physics when I was graduating, and during our last year at college we saw a good deal of each other. I've still got the woolen tam-o'-shanter she knitted so that I wouldn't bump my head against my space helmet. (No, I never had the nerve to wear it.)

Unfortunately, when I was assigned to Satellite Two Julie went to the Solar Observatory—at the same distance from Earth, but a couple of degrees eastward along the orbit. So there we were, sitting twenty-two thousand miles above the middle of Africa—but with nine hundred miles of empty, hostile space between us.

At first we were both so busy that the pang of separation was somewhat lessened. But when the novelty of life in space had worn off, our thoughts began to bridge the gulf that divided us. And not only our thoughts, for I'd made friends with the communications people, and we used to have little chats over the intersection TV circuit. In some ways it made matters worse seeing each other face to face and never knowing just how many other people were looking in at the same time. There's not much privacy in a space station. . . .

Sometimes I'd focus one of our telescopes onto the distant, brilliant star of the observatory. In the crystal clarity of space, I could use enormous magnifications, and could see every detail of our neighbors' equipment—the solar telescopes, the pressurized spheres of the living quarters that housed the staff, the slim pencils of visiting ferry rockets that had climbed up from Earth. Very often there would be space-suited figures moving among the maze of apparatus, and I would strain my eyes in a hopeless attempt at identification. It's hard enough to recognize anyone in a space suit when you're only a few feet apart—but that didn't stop me from trying.

We'd resigned ourselves to waiting, with what patience we could muster, until our Earth leave was due in six months' time, when we had an unexpected stroke of luck. Less than half our tour of duty had passed when the head of the transport section suddenly announced that he was going outside with a butterfly net to catch meteors. He didn't become violent, but had to be shipped hastily back to Earth. I took over his job on a temporary basis and now had—in theory at least—the freedom of space.

There were ten of the little low-powered rocket scooters under my proud command, as well as four of the larger interstation shuttles used to ferry stores and personnel from orbit to orbit. I couldn't hope to borrow one of *those,* but after several weeks of careful organizing I was able to carry out the plan I'd conceived some two micro-seconds after being told I was now head of transport.

There's no need to tell how I juggled duty lists, cooked logs and fuel registers, and persuaded my colleagues to cover up for me. All that matters is that, about once a week, I would climb into my personal space suit, strap myself to the spidery framework of a Mark III Scooter, and drift away from the station at minimum power. When I was well clear, I'd go over to full throttle, and the tiny rocket motor would hustle me across the nine-hundred-mile gap to the observatory.

The trip took about thirty minutes, and the navigational requirements were elementary. I could see where I was going and where I'd come from, yet I don't mind admitting that I often felt—well, a trifle lonely—around the mid-point of the journey. There was no other solid matter within almost five hundred miles—and it looked an awfully long way down to Earth. It was a great help, at such moments, to tune the suit radio to the general service band, and to listen to all the back-chat between ships and stations.

At mid-flight I'd have to spin the scooter around and start braking, and ten minutes later the observatory would be close enough for its details to be visible to the unaided eye. Very shortly after that I'd drift up to a small, plastic pressure bubble that was in the process of being fitted out as a spectroscopic laboratory—and there would be Julie, waiting on the other side of the air lock. . . .

I won't pretend that we confined our discussions to the latest results in astrophysics, or the progress of the satellite construction schedule. Few things, indeed, were further from our thoughts; and the journey home always seemed to flash by at a quite astonishing speed.

It was around mid-orbit on one of those homeward trips that the radar started to flash on my little control panel. There was something large at extreme range, and it was coming in fast. A meteor, I told myself—maybe even a small asteroid. Anything giving such a signal should be visible to the eye: I read off the bearings and searched the star fields in the indicated direction. The thought of a collision never even crossed my mind; space is so inconceivably vast that I was thousands of times safer than a man crossing a busy street on Earth.

There it was—a bright and steadily growing star near the foot of Orion. It already outshone Rigel, and seconds later it was not merely a star, but had begun to show a visible disk. Now it was moving as fast as I could turn my head; it grew to a tiny, misshaped moon, then dwindled and shrank with the same silent, inexorable speed.

I suppose I had a clear view of it for perhaps half a second, and that half-second has haunted me all my life. The—object—had already vanished by the time I thought of checking the radar again, so I had no way of gauging how close it came, and hence how large it really was. It could have been a small object a hundred feet away—or a very large one, ten miles off. There is no sense of perspective in space, and unless you know what you are looking at, you cannot judge its distance.

Of course, it *could* have been a very large and oddly shaped meteor; I can never be sure that my eyes, straining to grasp the details of so swiftly moving an object, were not hopelessly deceived. I may have imagined that I saw that broken, crumpled prow, and the cluster of dark ports like the sightless sockets of a skull. Of one thing only was I certain, even in that brief and fragmentary vision. If it *was* a ship, it was not one of ours. Its shape was utterly alien, and it was very, very old.

It may be that the greatest discovery of all time slipped from my grasp as I struggled with my thoughts midway between the two space stations. But I had no measurements of speed or direction; whatever it was that I had glimpsed was now lost beyond recapture in the wastes of the solar system.

What should I have done? No one would ever have believed me, for I would have had no proof. Had I made a report, there would have been endless trouble. I should have become the laughingstock of the Space Service, would have been reprimanded for misuse of equipment—and would certainly not have been able to see Julie again. And to me, at that age, nothing else was as important. If you've been in love yourself, you'll understand; if not, then no explanation is any use.

So I said nothing. To some other man (how many centuries hence?) will go the fame for proving that we were not the first-born of the children of the sun. Whatever it may be that is circling out there on its eternal orbit can wait, as it has waited ages already.

Yet I sometimes wonder. Would I have made a report, after all—had I known that Julie was going to marry someone else?

## The Call of the Stars

DOWN THERE on Earth the twentieth century is dying. As I look across at the shadowed globe blocking the stars, I can see the lights of a hundred sleepless cities, and there are moments when I wish that I could be among the crowds now surging and singing in the streets of London, Capetown, Rome, Paris, Berlin, Madrid. . . . Yes, I can see them all at a single glance, burning like fireflies against the darkened planet. The line of midnight is now bisecting Europe: in the eastern Mediterranean a tiny, brilliant star is pulsing as some exuberant pleasure ship waves her searchlights to the sky. I think she is deliberately aiming at us; for the past few minutes the flashes have been quite regular and startlingly bright. Presently I'll call the communications center and find out who she is, so that I can radio back our own greetings.

Passing into history now, receding forever down the stream of time, is the most incredible hundred years the world has ever seen. It opened with the conquest of the air, saw at its mid-point the unlocking of the atom—and now ends with the bridging of space.

(For the past five minutes I've been wondering what's happening to Nairobi; now I realize that they are putting on a mammoth fireworks display. Chemically fueled rockets may be obsolete out here—but they're still using lots of them down on Earth tonight.)

The end of a century—and the end of a millennium. What will the hundred years that begin with two and zero bring? The planets, of course; floating there in space, only a mile away, are the ships of the first Martian expedition. For two years I have watched them grow, assembled piece by piece, as the space station itself was built by the men I worked with a generation ago.

Those ten ships are ready now, with all their crews aboard, waiting for the final instrument check and the signal for departure. Before the first day of the new century has passed its noon, they will be tearing free from the reins of Earth, to head out toward the strange world that may one day be man's second home.

As I look at the brave little fleet that is now preparing to challenge infinity, my mind goes back forty years, to the days when the first satellites were launched and the moon still seemed very far away. And I remember—indeed, I have never forgotten—my father's fight to keep me down on Earth.

There were not many weapons he had failed to use. Ridicule had been the first: "Of course they can do it," he had sneered, "but what's the point? Who wants to go out into space while there's so much to be done here on Earth? There's not a single planet in the solar system where men can live. The moon's a burnt-out slag heap, and everywhere else is even worse. *This* is where we were meant to live."

Even then (I must have been eighteen or so at the time) I could tangle him up in points of logic. I can remember answering, "How do you know where we were meant to live, Dad? After all, we were in the sea for about a billion years before we decided to tackle the land. Now we're making the next big jump: I don't know where it will lead—nor did that first fish when it crawled up on the beach, and started to sniff the air."

So when he couldn't outargue me, he had tried subtler pressures. He was always talking about the dangers of space travel, and the short working life of anyone foolish enough to get involved in rocketry. At that time, people were still scared of meteors and cosmic rays; like the "Here Be Dragons" of the old map makers, they were the mythical monsters on the still-blank celestial charts. But they didn't worry me; if anything, they added the spice of danger to my dreams.

While I was going through college, Father was comparatively quiet. My training would be valuable whatever profession I took up in later life, so he could not complain —though he occasionally grumbled about the money I wasted buying all the books and magazines on astronautics that I could find. My college record was good, which naturally pleased him; perhaps he did not realize that it would also help me to get my way.

All through my final year I had avoided talking of my plans. I had even given the impression (though I am sorry for that now) that I had abandoned my dream of going into space. Without saying anything to him, I put in my application to Astrotech, and was accepted as soon as I had graduated.

The storm broke when that long blue envelope with the embossed heading "Institute of Astronautical Technology" dropped into the mailbox. I was accused of deceit and ingratitude, and I do not think I ever forgave my father for destroying the pleasure I should have felt at being chosen for the most exclusive—and most glamorous—apprenticeship the world has ever known.

The vacations were an ordeal; had it not been for Mother's sake, I do not think I would have gone home more than once a year, and I always left again as quickly as I could. I had hoped that Father would mellow as my training progressed and as he accepted the inevitable, but he never did.

Then had come that stiff and awkward parting at the space-port, with the rain streaming down from leaden skies and beating against the smooth walls of the ship that seemed so eagerly waiting to climb into the eternal sunlight beyond the reach of storms. I know now what it cost my father to watch the machine he hated swallow up his only son: for I understand many things today that were hidden from me then.

He knew, even as we parted at the ship, that he would never see me again. Yet his old, stubborn pride kept him from saying the only words that might have held me back. I knew that he was ill, but how ill, he had told no one. That was the only weapon he had not used against me, and I respect him for it.

Would I have stayed had I known? It is even more futile to speculate about the unchangeable past than the unforeseeable future; all I can say now is that I am glad I never had to make the choice. At the end he let me go; he gave up his fight against my ambition, and a little while later his fight with Death.

So I said good-by to Earth, and to the father who loved me but knew no way to say it. He lies down there on the planet I can cover with my hand; how strange it is to think that of the countless billion human beings whose blood runs in my veins, I was the very first to leave his native world. . . .

The new day is breaking over Asia; a hairline of fire is rimming the eastern edge of Earth. Soon it will grow into a burning crescent as the sun comes up out of the Pacific —yet Europe is preparing for sleep, except for those revelers who will stay up to greet the dawn.

And now, over there by the flagship, the ferry rocket is coming back for the last visitors from the station. Here comes the message I have been waiting for: CAPTAIN STEVENS

PRESENTS HIS COMPLIMENTS TO THE STATION COMMANDER.
BLAST-OFF WILL BE IN NINETY MINUTES; HE WILL BE GLAD
TO SEE YOU ABOARD NOW.

Well, Father, now I know how you felt: time has gone
full circle. Yet I hope that I have learned from the mistakes
we both made, long ago. I shall remember you when I go
over there to the flagship *Starfire* and say good-by to the
grandson you never knew.

## THE WALL OF DARKNESS

MANY AND STRANGE are the universes that drift like bubbles
in the foam upon the River of Time. Some—a very few—
move against or athwart its current; and fewer still are those
that lie forever beyond its reach, knowing nothing of the
future or the past. Shervane's tiny cosmos was not one of
these: its strangeness was of a different order. It held one
world only—the planet of Shervane's race—and a single star,
the great sun Trilorne that brought it life and light.

Shervane knew nothing of night, for Trilorne was always
high above the horizon, dipping near it only in the long
months of winter. Beyond the borders of the Shadow Land,
it was true, there came a season when Trilorne disappeared
below the edge of the world, and a darkness fell in which
nothing could live. But even then the darkness was not
absolute, though there were no stars to relieve it.

Alone in its little cosmos, turning the same face always
toward its solitary sun, Shervane's world was the last and the
strangest jest of the Maker of the Stars.

Yet as he looked across his father's lands, the thoughts
that filled Shervane's mind were those that any human child
might have known. He felt awe, and curiosity, and a little
fear, and above all a longing to go out into the great world
before him. These things he was still too young to do, but
the ancient house was on the highest ground for many miles
and he could look far out over the land that would one day
be his. When he turned to the north, with Trilorne shining
full upon his face, he could see many miles away the long
line of mountains that curved around to the right, rising
higher and higher, until they disappeared behind him in the

direction of the Shadow Land. One day, when he was older, he would go through those mountains along the pass that led to the great lands of the east.

On his left was the ocean, only a few miles away, and sometimes Shervane could hear the thunder of the waves as they fought and tumbled on the gently sloping sands. No one knew how far the ocean reached. Ships had set out across it, sailing northward while Trilorne rose higher and higher in the sky and the heat of its rays grew ever more intense. Long before the great sun had reached the zenith, they had been forced to return. If the mythical Fire Lands did indeed exist, no man could ever hope to reach their burning shores—unless the legends were really true. Once, it was said, there had been swift metal ships that could cross the ocean despite the heat of Trilorne, and so come to the lands on the other side of the world. Now these countries could be reached only by a tedious journey over land and sea, which could be shortened no more than a little by traveling as far north as one dared.

All the inhabited countries of Shervane's world lay in the narrow belt between burning heat and insufferable cold. In every land, the far north was an unapproachable region smitten by the fury of Trilorne. And to the south of all countries lay the vast and gloomy Shadow Land, where Trilorne was never more than a pale disk on the horizon, and often was not visible at all.

These things Shervane learned in the years of his childhood, and in those years he had no wish to leave the wide lands between the mountains and the sea. Since the dawn of time his ancestors and the races before them had toiled to make these lands the fairest in the world; if they had failed, it was by a narrow margin. There were gardens bright with strange flowers, there were streams that trickled gently between moss-grown rocks to be lost in the pure waters of the tideless sea. There were fields of grain that rustled continually in the wind, as if the generations of seeds yet unborn were talking one to the other. In the wide meadows and beneath the trees the friendly cattle wandered aimlessly with foolish cries. And there was the great house, with its enormous rooms and its endless corridors, vast enough in reality but huger still to the mind of a child. This was the world he knew and loved. As yet, what lay beyond its borders had not concerned his mind.

But Shervane's universe was not one of those free from the domination of time. The harvest ripened and was gathered into the granaries; Trilorne rocked slowly through its little arc of sky, and with the passing seasons Shervane's mind and body grew. His land seemed smaller now: the mountains were nearer and the sea was only a brief walk from the great house. He began to learn of the world in which he lived, and to be made ready for the part he must play in its shaping.

Some of these things he learned from his father, Sherval, but most he was taught by Grayle, who had come across the mountains in the days of his father's father, and had now been tutor to three generations of Shervane's family. He was fond of Grayle, though the old man taught him many things he had no wish to learn, and the years of his boyhood passed pleasantly enough until the time came for him to go through the mountains into the lands beyond. Ages ago his family had come from the great countries of the east, and in every generation since, the eldest son had made that pilgrimage again to spend a year of his youth among his cousins. It was a wise custom, for beyond the mountains much of the knowledge of the past still lingered, and there one could meet men from other lands and study their ways.

In the last spring before his son's departure, Sherval collected three of his servants and certain animals it is convenient to call horses, and took Shervane to see those parts of the land he had never visited before. They rode west to the sea, and followed it for many days, until Trilorne was noticeably nearer the horizon. Still they went south, their shadows lengthening before them, turning again to the east only when the rays of the sun seemed to have lost all their power. They were now well within the limits of the Shadow Land, and it would not be wise to go farther south until the summer was at its height.

Shervane was riding beside his father, watching the changing landscape with all the eager curiosity of a boy seeing a new country for the first time. His father was talking about the soil, describing the crops that could be grown here and those that would fail if the attempt were made. But Shervane's attention was elsewhere: he was staring out across the desolate Shadow Land, wondering how far it stretched and what mysteries it held.

"Father," he said presently, "if you went south in a straight line, right across the Shadow Land, would you reach the other side of the world?"

His father smiled.

"Men have asked that question for centuries," he said, "but there are two reasons why they will never know the answer."

"What are they?"

"The first, of course, is the darkness and the cold. Even

here, nothing can live during the winter months. But there is a better reason, though I see that Grayle has not spoken of it."

"I don't think he has: at least, I do not remember."

For a moment Sherval did not reply. He stood up in his stirrups and surveyed the land to the south.

"Once I knew this place well," he said to Shervane. "Come —I have something to show you."

They turned away from the path they had been following, and for several hours rode once more with their backs to the sun. The land was rising slowly now, and Shervane saw that they were climbing a great ridge of rock that pointed like a dagger into the heart of the Shadow Land. They came presently to a hill too steep for the horses to ascend, and here they dismounted and left the animals in the servants' charge.

"There is a way around," said Sherval, "but it is quicker for us to climb than to take the horses to the other side."

The hill, though steep, was only a small one, and they reached its summit in a few minutes. At first Shervane could see nothing he had not met before; there was only the same undulating wilderness, which seemed to become darker and more forbidding with every yard that its distance from Trilorne increased.

He turned to his father with some bewilderment, but Sherval pointed to the far south and drew a careful line along the horizon.

"It is not easy to see," he said quietly. "My father showed it to me from this same spot, many years before you were born."

Shervane stared into the dusk. The southern sky was so dark as to be almost black, and it came down to meet the edge of the world. But not quite, for along the horizon, in a great curve dividing land from sky yet seeming to belong to neither, was a band of deeper darkness, black as the night which Shervane had never known.

He looked at it steadfastly for a long time, and perhaps some hint of the future may have crept into his soul, for the darkling land seemed suddenly alive and waiting. When at last he tore his eyes away, he knew that nothing would ever be the same again, though he was still too young to recognize the challenge for what it was.

And so, for the first time in his life, Shervane saw the Wall.

In the early spring he said farewell to his people, and went with one servant over the mountains into the great lands of the eastern world. Here he met the men who shared his ancestry, and here he studied the history of his race, the arts that had grown from ancient times, and the sciences that ruled the lives of men. In the places of learning he made friends with boys who had come from lands even farther to the east: few of these was he likely to see again, but one was to play a greater part in his life than either could have imagined. Brayldon's father was a famous architect, but his son intended to eclipse him. He was traveling from land to land, always learning, watching, asking questions. Though he was only a few years older than Shervane, his knowledge of the world was infinitely greater—or so it seemed to the younger boy.

Between them they took the world to pieces and rebuilt it according to their desires. Brayldon dreamed of cities whose great avenues and stately towers would shame even the wonders of the past, but Shervane's interests lay more with the people who would dwell in those cities, and the way they ordered their lives.

They often spoke of the Wall, which Brayldon knew from the stories of his own people, though he himself had never seen it. Far to the south of every country, as Shervane had learned, it lay like a great barrier athwart the Shadow Land. In high summer it could be reached, though only with difficulty, but nowhere was there any way of passing it, and none knew what lay beyond. An entire world, never pausing even when it reached a hundred times the height of a man, it encircled the wintry sea that washed the shores of the Shadow Land. Travelers had stood upon those lonely beaches, scarcely warmed by the last thin rays of Trilorne, and had seen how the dark shadow of the Wall marched out to sea contemptuous of the waves beneath its feet. And on the far shores, other travelers had watched it come striding in across the ocean, to sweep past them on its journey round the world.

"One of my uncles," said Brayldon, "one reached the Wall when he was a young man. He did it for a wager, and he rode for ten days before he came beneath it. I think it frightened him—it was so huge and cold. He could not tell whether it was made of metal or of stone, and when he shouted, there was no echo at all, but his voice died away quickly as if the Wall were swallowing the sound. My people believe it is the end of the world, and there is nothing beyond."

"If that were true," Shervane replied, with irrefutable logic, "the ocean would have poured over the edge before the Wall was built."

"Not if Kyrone built it when He made the world."

Shervane did not agree.

"*My* people believe it is the work of man—perhaps the engineers of the First Dynasty, who made so many wonderful things. If they really had ships that could reach the Fire Lands—and even ships that could fly—they might have possessed enough wisdom to build the Wall."

Brayldon shrugged.

"They must have had a very good reason," he said. "We can never know the answer, so why worry about it?"

This eminently practical advice, as Shervane had discovered, was all that the ordinary man ever gave him. Only philosophers were interested in unanswerable questions: to most people, the enigma of the Wall, like the problem of existence itself, was something that scarcely concerned their minds. And all the philosophers he had met had given him different answers.

First there had been Grayle, whom he had questioned on his return from the Shadow Land. The old man had looked at him quietly and said:

"There is only one thing behind the Wall, so I have heard. And that is madness."

Then there had been Artex, who was so old that he could scarcely hear Shervane's nervous questioning. He gazed at the boy through eyelids that seemed too tired to open fully, and had replied after a long time:

"Kyrone built the Wall in the third day of the making of the world. What is beyond, we shall discover when we die—for there go the souls of all the dead."

Yet Irgan, who lived in the same city, had flatly contradicted this.

"Only memory can answer your question, my son. For behind the Wall is the land in which we lived before our births."

Whom could he believe? The truth was that no one knew: if the knowledge had ever been possessed, it had been lost ages since.

Though this quest was unsuccessful, Shervane had learned many things in his year of study. With the returning spring he said farewell to Brayldon and the other friends he had known for such a little while, and set out along the ancient road that led him back to his own country. Once again he made the perilous journey through the great pass between the mountains, where walls of ice hung threatening against the sky. He came to the place where the road curved down once more toward the world of men, where there was warmth and running water and the breath no longer labored in the freezing air. Here, on the last rise of the road before it descended into the valley, one could see far out across the land to the distant gleam of the ocean. And there, almost lost in the mists at the edge of the world, Shervane could see the line of shadow that was his own country.

He went on down the great ribbon of stone until he came to the bridge that men had built across the cataract in the ancient days when the only other way had been destroyed by earthquake. But the bridge was gone: the storms and avalanches of early spring had swept away one of the mighty piers, and the beautiful metal rainbow lay a twisted ruin in the spray and foam a thousand feet below. The summer would have come and gone before the road could be opened once more: as Shervane sadly returned he knew that another year must pass ere he would see his home again.

He paused for many minutes on the last curve of the road, looking back toward the unattainable land that held all the things he loved. But the mists had closed over it, and he saw it no more. Resolutely he turned back along the road until the open lands had vanished and the mountains enfolded him again.

Brayldon was still in the city when Shervane returned. He was surprised and pleased to see his friend, and together they discussed what should be done in the year ahead. Shervane's cousins, who had grown fond of their guest, were not sorry to see him again, but their kindly suggestion that he should devote another year to study was not well received.

Shervane's plan matured slowly, in the face of considerable opposition. Even Brayldon was not enthusiastic at first, and much argument was needed before he would co-operate. Thereafter, the agreement of everyone else who mattered was only a question of time.

Summer was approaching when the two boys set out toward Brayldon's country. They rode swiftly, for the journey was a long one and must be completed before Trilorne began its winter fall. When they reached the lands that Brayldon knew, they made certain inquiries which caused much shaking of heads. But the answers they obtained were accurate, and soon the Shadow Land was all around them, and presently for the second time in his life Shervane saw the Wall.

It seemed not far away when they first came upon it, rising from a bleak and lonely plain. Yet they rode endlessly across that plain before the Wall grew any nearer—and then they had almost reached its base before they realized how close they were, for there was no way of judging its distance until one could reach out and touch it.

When Shervane gazed up at the monstrous ebony sheet that had so troubled his mind, it seemed to be overhanging and about to crush him beneath its falling weight. With difficulty, he tore his eyes away from the hypnotic sight, and went nearer to examine the material of which the Wall was built.

It was true, as Brayldon had told him, that it felt cold to the touch—colder than it had any right to be even in this sun-starved land. It felt neither hard nor soft, for its texture eluded the hand in a way that was difficult to analyze. Shervane had the impression that something was preventing him from actual contact with the surface, yet he could see no space between the Wall and his fingers when he forced them against it. Strangest of all was the uncanny silence of which Brayldon's uncle had spoken: every word was deadened and all sounds died away with unnatural swiftness.

Brayldon had unloaded some tools and instruments from the pack horses, and had begun to examine the Wall's surface. He found very quickly that no drills or cutters would mark it in any way, and presently he came to the conclusion Shervane had already reached. The Wall was not merely adamant: it was unapproachable.

At last, in disgust, he took a perfectly straight metal rule and pressed its edge against the wall. While Shervane held a mirror to reflect the feeble light of Trilorne along the line of contact, Brayldon peered at the rule from the other side. It was as he had thought: an infinitely narrow streak of light showed unbroken between the two surfaces.

Brayldon looked thoughtfully at his friend.

"Shervane," he said, "I don't believe the Wall is made of matter, as we know it."

"Then perhaps the legends were right that said it was never built at all, but created as we see it now."

"I think so too," said Brayldon. "The engineers of the First Dynasty had such powers. There are some very ancient buildings in my land that seem to have been made in a single operation from a substance that shows absolutely no sign of weathering. If it were black instead of colored, it would be very much like the material of the Wall."

He put away his useless tools and began to set up a simple portable theodolite.

"If I can do nothing else," he said with a wry smile, "at least I can find exactly how high it is!"

When they looked back for their last view of the Wall,

Shervane wondered if he would ever see it again. There was nothing more he could learn: for the future, he must forget this foolish dream that he might one day master its secret. Perhaps there was no secret at all—perhaps beyond the Wall the Shadow Land stretched round the curve of the world until it met that same barrier again. That, surely, seemed the likeliest thing. But if it were so, then why had the Wall been built, and by what race?

With an almost angry effort of will, he put these thoughts aside and rode forward into the light of Trilorne, thinking of a future in which the Wall would play no more part than it did in the lives of other men.

So two years had passed before Shervane could return to his home. In two years, especially when one is young, much can be forgotten and even the things nearest to the heart lose their distinctness, so that they can no longer be clearly recalled. When Shervane came through the last foothills of the mountains and was again in the country of his childhood, the joy of his home-coming was mingled with a strange sadness. So many things were forgotten that he had once thought his mind would hold forever.

The news of his return had gone before him, and soon he saw far ahead a line of horses galloping along the road. He pressed forward eagerly, wondering if Sherval would be there to greet him, and was a little disappointed when he saw that Grayle was leading the procession.

Shervane halted as the old man rode up to his horse. Then Grayle put his hand upon his shoulder, but for a while he turned away his head and could not speak.

And presently Shervane learned that the storms of the year before had destroyed more than the ancient bridge, for the lightning had brought his own home in ruins to the ground. Years before the appointed time, all the lands that Sherval had owned had passed into the possession of his son. Far more, indeed, than these, for the whole family had been assembled, according to its yearly custom, in the great house when the fire had come down upon it. In a single moment of time, everything between the mountains and the sea had passed into his keeping. He was the richest man his land had known for generations; and all these things he would have given to look again into the calm gray eyes of the father he would see no more.

Trilorne had risen and fallen in the sky many times since Shervane took leave of his childhood on the road before the mountains. The land had flourished in the passing years, and the possessions that had so suddenly become his had steadily increased their value. He had husbanded them well, and now he had time once more in which to dream. More than that— he had the wealth to make his dreams come true.

Often stories had come across the mountains of the work Brayldon was doing in the east, and although the two friends had never met since their youth they had exchanged messages regularly. Brayldon had achieved his ambitions: not only had he designed the two largest buildings erected since the ancient days, but a whole new city had been planned by him, though it would not be completed in his lifetime. Hearing of these things, Shervane remembered the aspirations of his own youth, and his mind went back across the years to the day when they had stood together beneath the majesty of the Wall. For a long time he wrestled with his thoughts, fearing to revive old longings that might not be assuaged. But at last he made his decision and wrote to Brayldon—for what was the use of wealth and power unless they could be used to shape one's dreams?

Then Shervane waited, wondering if Brayldon had forgotten the past in the years that had brought him fame. He had not long to wait: Brayldon could not come at once, for he had great works to carry to their completion, but when they were finished he would join his old friend. Shervane had thrown him a challenge that was worthy of his skill—one which if he could meet would bring him more satisfaction than anything he had yet done.

Early the next summer he came, and Shervane met him on the road below the bridge. They had been boys when they last parted, and now they were nearing middle age, yet as they greeted one another the years seemed to fall away and each was secretly glad to see how lightly Time had touched the friend he remembered.

They spent many days in conference together, considering the plans that Brayldon had drawn up. The work was an immense one, and would take many years to complete, but it was possible to a man of Shervane's wealth. Before he gave his final assent, he took his friend to see Grayle.

The old man had been living for some years in the little house that Shervane had built him. For a long time he had played no active part in the life of the great estates, but his advice was always ready when it was needed, and it was invariably wise.

Grayle knew why Brayldon had come to this land, and

he expressed no surprise when the architect unrolled his sketches. The largest drawing showed the elevation of the Wall, with a great stairway rising along its side from the plain beneath. At six equally spaced intervals the slowly ascending ramp leveled out into wide platforms, the last of which was only a short distance below the summit of the Wall. Springing from the stairway at a score of places along its length were flying buttresses which to Grayle's eye seemed very frail and slender for the work they had to do. Then he realized that the great ramp would be largely self-supporting, and on one side all the lateral thrust would be taken by the Wall itself.

He looked at the drawing in silence for a while, and then remarked quietly:

"You always managed to have your way, Shervane. I might have guessed that this would happen in the end."

"Then you think it a good idea?" Shervane asked. He had never gone against the old man's advice, and was anxious to have it now. As usual Grayle came straight to the point.

"How much will it cost?" he said.

Brayldon told him, and for a moment there was a shocked silence.

"That includes," the architect said hastily, "the building of a good road across the Shadow Land, and the construction of a small town for the workmen. The stairway itself is made from about a million identical blocks which can be dovetailed together to form a rigid structure. We shall make these, I hope, from the minerals we find in the Shadow Land."

He sighed a little.

"I should have liked to have built it from metal rods, jointed together, but that would have cost even more, for all the material would have to be brought over the mountains."

Grayle examined the drawing more closely.

"Why have you stopped short of the top?" he asked.

Brayldon looked at Shervane, who answered the question with a trace of embarrassment.

"I want to be the only one to make the final ascent," he replied. "The last stage will be a lifting machine on the highest platform. There may be danger: that is why I am going alone."

That was not the only reason, but it was a good one. Behind the Wall, so Grayle had once said, lay madness. If that were true, no one else need face it.

Grayle was speaking once more in his quiet, dreamy voice.

"In that case," he said, "what you do is neither good nor

bad, for it concerns you alone. If the Wall was built to keep something from our world, it will still be impassable from the other side."

Brayldon nodded.

"We had thought of that," he said with a touch of pride. "If the need should come, the ramp can be destroyed in a moment by explosives at selected spots."

"That is good," the old man replied. "Though I do not believe those stories, it is well to be prepared. When the work is finished, I hope I shall still be here. And now I shall try to remember what I heard of the Wall when I was as young as you were, Shervane, when you first questioned me about it."

Before the winter came, the road to the Wall had been marked out and the foundations of the temporary town had been laid. Most of the materials Brayldon needed were not hard to find, for the Shadow Land was rich in minerals. He had also surveyed the Wall itself and chosen the spot for the stairway. When Trilorne began to dip below the horizon, Brayldon was well content with the work that had been done.

By the next summer the first of the myriad concrete blocks had been made and tested to Brayldon's satisfaction, and before winter came again some thousands had been produced and part of the foundations laid. Leaving a trusted assistant in charge of the production, Brayldon could now return to his interrupted work. When enough of the blocks had been made, he would be back to supervise the building, but until then his guidance would not be needed.

Two or three times in the course of every year, Shervane rode out to the Wall to watch the stockpiles growing into great pyramids, and four years later Brayldon returned with him. Layer by layer the lines of stone started to creep up the flanks of the Wall, and the slim buttresses began to arch out into space. At first the stairway rose slowly, but as its summit narrowed the increase became more and more rapid. For a third of every year the work had to be abandoned, and there were anxious months in the long winter when Shervane stood on the borders of the Shadow Land, listening to the storms that thundered past him into the reverberating darkness. But Brayldon had built well, and every spring the work was standing unharmed as though it would outlive the Wall itself.

The last stones were laid seven years after the beginning of the work. Standing a mile away, so that he could see the structure in its entirety, Shervane remembered with wonder how all this had sprung from the few sketches Brayldon had shown him years ago, and he knew something of the emotion the artist must feel when his dreams become reality. And he remembered, too, the day when, as a boy by his father's side, he had first seen the Wall far off against the dusky sky of the Shadow Land.

There were guardrails around the upper platform, but Shervane did not care to go near its edge. The ground was at a dizzying distance, and he tried to forget his height by helping Brayldon and the workmen erect the simple hoist that would lift him the remaining twenty feet. When it was ready he stepped into the machine and turned to his friend with all the assurance he could muster.

"I shall be gone only a few minutes," he said with elaborate casualness. "Whatever I find, I'll return immediately."

He could hardly have guessed how small a choice was his.

Grayle was now almost blind and would not know another spring. But he recognized the approaching footsteps and greeted Brayldon by name before his visitor had time to speak.

"I am glad you came," he said. "I've been thinking of everything you told me, and I believe I know the truth at last. Perhaps you have guessed it already."

"No," said Brayldon. "I have been afraid to think of it." The old man smiled a little.

"Why should one be afraid of something merely because it is strange? The Wall is wonderful, yes—but there's nothing terrible about it, to those who will face its secret without flinching.

"When I was a boy, Brayldon, my old master once said that time could never destroy the truth—it could only hide it among legends. He was right. From all the fables that have gathered around the Wall, I can now select the ones that are part of history.

"Long ago, Brayldon, when the First Dynasty was at its height, Trilorne was hotter than it is now and the Shadow Land was fertile and inhabited—as perhaps one day the Fire Lands may be when Trilorne is old and feeble. Men could go southward as they pleased, for there was no Wall to bar the way. Many must have done so, looking for new lands in which to settle. What happened to Shervane happened to them also, and it must have wrecked many minds—so many that the scientists of the First Dynasty built the Wall to prevent madness from spreading through the land. I cannot believe that this is true, but the legend says that it was made in a single day, with no labor, out of a cloud that encircled the world."

He fell into a reverie, and for a moment Brayldon did not disturb him. His mind was far in the past, picturing his world as a perfect globe floating in space while the Ancient Ones threw the band of darkness around the equator. False though that picture was in its most important detail, he could never wholly erase it from his mind.

•

As the last few feet of the Wall moved slowly past his eyes, Shervane needed all his courage lest he cry out to be lowered again. He remembered certain terrible stories he had once dismissed with laughter, for he came of a race that was singularly free from superstition. But what if, after all, those stories had been true, and the Wall had been built to keep some horror from the world?

He tried to forget these thoughts, and found it not hard to do so once he had passed the topmost level of the Wall. At first he could not interpret the picture his eyes brought him: then he saw that he was looking across an unbroken black sheet whose width he could not judge.

The little platform came to a stop, and he noted with half-conscious admiration how accurate Brayldon's calculations had been. Then, with a last word of assurance to the group below, he stepped onto the Wall and began to walk steadily forward.

At first it seemed as if the plain before him was infinite, for he could not even tell where it met the sky. But he walked on unfaltering, keeping his back to Trilorne. He wished he could have used his own shadow as a guide, but it was lost in the deeper darkness beneath his feet.

There was something wrong: it was growing darker with every footstep he took. Startled, he turned around and saw that the disk of Trilorne had now become pale and dusky, as if seen through a darkened glass. With mounting fear, he realized that this was by no means all that had happened— *Trilorne was smaller than the sun he had known all his life.*

He shook his head in an angry gesture of defiance. These things were fancies; he was imagining them. Indeed, they were so contrary to all experience that somehow he no longer felt frightened but strode resolutely forward with only a glance at the sun behind.

When Trilorne had dwindled to a point, and the darkness was all around him, it was time to abandon pretense. A wiser man would have turned back there and then, and Shervane had a sudden nightmare vision of himself lost in this eternal twilight between earth and sky, unable to retrace the path that led to safety. Then he remembered that as long as he could see Trilorne at all he could be in no real danger.

A little uncertainly now, he continued his way with many backward glances at the faint guiding light behind him. Trilorne itself had vanished, but there was still a dim glow in the sky to mark its place. And presently he needed its aid no longer, for far ahead a second light was appearing in the heavens.

At first it seemed only the faintest of glimmers, and when he was sure of its existence he noticed that Trilorne had already disappeared. But he felt more confidence now, and as he moved onward, the returning light did something to subdue his fears.

When he saw that he was indeed approaching another sun, when he could tell beyond any doubt that it was expanding as a moment ago he had seen Trilorne contract, he forced all amazement down into the depths of his mind. He would only observe and record: later there would be time to understand these things. That his world might possess two suns, one shining upon it from either side, was not, after all, beyond imagination.

Now at last he could see, faintly through the darkness, the ebon line that marked the Wall's other rim. Soon he would be the first man in thousands of years, perhaps in eternity, to look upon the lands that it had sundered from his world. Would they be as fair as his own, and would there be people there whom he would be glad to greet?

But that they would be waiting, and in such a way, was more than he had dreamed.

Grayle stretched his hand out toward the cabinet beside him and fumbled for a large sheet of paper that was lying upon it. Brayldon watched him in silence, and the old man continued.

"How often we have all heard arguments about the size of the universe, and whether it has any boundaries! We can imagine no ending to space, yet our minds rebel at the idea of infinity. Some philosophers have imagined that space is limited by curvature in a higher dimension—I suppose you know the theory. It may be true of other universes, if they exist, but for ours the answer is more subtle.

"*Along the line of the Wall, Brayldon, our universe comes to an end—and yet does not.* There was no boundary, nothing to stop one going onward before the Wall was built. The

Wall itself is merely a man-made barrier, sharing the properties of the space in which it lies. Those properties were
always there, and the Wall added nothing to them."

He held the sheet of paper toward Brayldon and slowly
rotated it.

"Here," he said, "is a plain sheet. It has, of course, two
sides. *Can you imagine one that has not?*"

Brayldon stared at him in amazement.

"That's impossible—ridiculous!"

"But is it?" said Grayle softly. He reached toward the
cabinet again and his fingers groped in its recesses. Then he
drew out a long, flexible strip of paper and turned vacant
eyes to the silently waiting Brayldon.

"We cannot match the intellects of the First Dynasty, but
what their minds could grasp directly we can approach by
analogy. This simple trick, which seems so trivial, may help
you to glimpse the truth."

He ran his fingers along the paper strip, then joined the
two ends together to make a circular loop.

"Here I have a shape which is perfectly familiar to you—
the section of a cylinder. I run my finger around the inside,
so—and now along the outside. The two surfaces are quite
distinct: you can go from one to the other only by moving
through the thickness of the strip. Do you agree?"

"Of course," said Brayldon, still puzzled. "But what does
it prove?"

"Nothing," said Grayle. "But now watch—"

This sun, Shervane thought, was Trilorne's identical twin.
The darkness had now lifted completely, and there was no
longer the sensation, which he would not try to understand,
of walking across an infinite plain.

He was moving slowly now, for he had no desire to come
too suddenly upon that vertiginous precipice. In a little while
he could see a distant horizon of low hills, as bare and lifeless as those he had left behind him. This did not disappoint
him unduly, for the first glimpse of his own land would be
no more attractive than this.

So he walked on: and when presently an icy hand fastened
itself upon his heart, he did not pause as a man of lesser
courage would have done. Without flinching, he watched that
shockingly familiar landscape rise around him, until he could
see the plain from which his journey had started, and the
great stairway itself, and at last Brayldon's anxious, waiting
face.

Again Grayle brought the two ends of the strip together,

but now he had given it a half-twist so that the band was kinked. He held it out to Brayldon.

"Run your finger around it now," he said quietly.

Brayldon did not do so: he could see the old man's meaning.

"I understand," he said. "You no longer have two separate surfaces. It now forms a single continuous sheet—*a one-sided surface*—something that at first sight seems utterly impossible."

"Yes," replied Grayle very softly. "I thought you would understand. *A one-sided surface.* Perhaps you realize now why this symbol of the twisted loop is so common in the ancient religions, though its meaning has been completely lost. Of course, it is no more than a crude and simple analogy —an example in two dimensions of what must really occur in three. But it is as near as our minds can ever get to the truth."

There was a long, brooding silence. Then Grayle sighed deeply and turned to Brayldon as if he could still see his face.

"Why did you come back before Shervane?" he asked, though he knew the answer well enough.

"We had to do it," said Brayldon sadly, "but I did not wish to see my work destroyed."

Grayle nodded in sympathy.

"I understand," he said.

Shervane ran his eye up the long flight of steps on which no feet would ever tread again. He felt few regrets: he had striven, and no one could have done more. Such victory as was possible had been his.

Slowly he raised his hand and gave the signal. The Wall swallowed the explosion as it had absorbed all other sounds, but the unhurried grace with which the long tiers of masonry curtsied and fell was something he would remember all his life. For a moment he had a sudden, inexpressibly poignant vision of another stairway, watched by another Shervane, falling in identical ruins on the far side of the Wall.

But that, he realized, was a foolish thought: for none knew better than he that the Wall possessed no other side.

## SECURITY CHECK

IT IS OFTEN SAID that in our age of assembly lines and mass production there's no room for the individual craftsman, the artist in wood or metal who made so many of the treasures of the past. Like most generalizations, this simply isn't true. He's rarer now, of course, but he's certainly not extinct. He has often had to change his vocation, but in his modest way he still flourishes. Even on the island of Manhattan he may be found, if you know where to look for him. Where rents are low and fire regulations unheard of, his minute, cluttered workshops may be discovered in the basements of apartment houses or in the upper stories of derelict shops. He may no longer make violins or cuckoo clocks or music boxes, but the skills he uses are the same as they always were, and no two objects he creates are ever identical. He is not contemptuous of mechanization: you will find several electric hand tools under the debris on his bench. He has moved with the times: he will always be around, the universal odd-job man who is never aware of it when he makes an immortal work of art.

Hans Muller's workshop consisted of a large room at the back of a deserted warehouse, no more than a vigorous stone's throw from the Queensborough Bridge. Most of the building had been boarded up awaiting demolition, and sooner or later Hans would have to move. The only entrance was across a weed-covered yard used as a parking place during the day, and much frequented by the local juvenile delinquents at night. They had never given Hans any trouble, for he knew better than to co-operate with the police when they made their periodic inquiries. The police fully appreciated his delicate position and did not press matters, so Hans was on good terms with everybody. Being a peaceable citizen, that suited him very well.

The work on which Hans was now engaged would have deeply puzzled his Bavarian ancestors. Indeed, ten years ago it would have puzzled Hans himself. And it had all started because a bankrupt client had given him a TV set in payment for services rendered. . . .

Hans had accepted the offer reluctantly, not because he

was old-fashioned and disapproved of TV, but simply because he couldn't imagine where he would find time to look at the darned thing. Still, he thought, at least I can always sell it for fifty dollars. But before I do that, let's see what the programs are like. . . .

His hand had gone out to the switch: the screen had filled with moving shapes—and, like millions of men before him, Hans was lost. He entered a world he had not known existed —a world of battling spaceships, of exotic planets and strange races—the world, in fact, of Captain Zipp, Commander of the Space Legion.

Only when the tedious recital of the virtues of Crunche, the Wonder Cereal, had given way to an almost equally tedious boxing match between two muscle-bound characters who seemed to have signed a nonaggression pact, did the magic fade. Hans was a simple man. He had always been fond of fairy tales—and *this* was the modern fairy tale, with trimmings of which the Grimm Brothers had never dreamed. So Hans did not sell his TV set.

It was some weeks before the initial naïve, uncritical enjoyment wore off. The first thing that began to annoy Hans was the furniture and general décor in the world of the future. He was, as has been indicated, an artist—and he refused to believe that in a hundred years taste would have deteriorated as badly as the Crunche sponsors seemed to imagine.

He also thought very little of the weapons that Captain Zipp and his opponents used. It was true that Hans did not pretend to understand the principles upon which the portable proton disintegrator was based, but however it worked, there was certainly no reason why it should be *that* clumsy. The clothes, the spaceship interiors—they just weren't convincing. How did he know? He had always possessed a highly developed sense of the fitness of things, and it could still operate even in this novel field.

We have said that Hans was a simple man. He was also a shrewd one, and he had heard that there was money in TV. So he sat down and began to draw.

Even if the producer of Captain Zipp had not lost patience with his set designer, Hans Muller's ideas would certainly have made him sit up and take notice. There was an authenticity and realism about them that made them quite outstanding. They were completely free from the element of phonyness that had begun to upset even Captain Zipp's most juvenile followers. Hans was hired on the spot.

He made his own conditions, however. What he was doing

he did largely for love, notwithstanding the fact that it was earning him more money than anything he had ever done before in his life. He would take no assistants, and would remain in his little workshop. All that he wanted to do was to produce the prototypes, the basic designs. The mass production could be done somewhere else—he was a craftsman, not a factory.

The arrangement had worked well. Over the last six months Captain Zipp had been transformed and was now the despair of all the rival space operas. This, his viewers thought, was not just a serial about the future. It *was* the future—there was no argument about it. Even the actors seemed to have been inspired by their new surroundings: off the set, they sometimes behaved like twentieth-century time travelers stranded in the Victorian Age, indignant because they no longer had access to the gadgets that had always been part of their lives.

But Hans knew nothing about this. He toiled happily away, refusing to see anyone except the producer, doing all his business over the telephone—and watching the final result to ensure that his ideas had not been mutilated. The only sign of his connection with the slightly fantastic world of commercial TV was a crate of Crunche in one corner of the workshop. He had sampled one mouthful of this present from the grateful sponsor and had then remembered thankfully that, after all, he was not paid to eat the stuff.

He was working late one Sunday evening, putting the final touches to a new design for a space helmet, when he suddenly realized that he was no longer alone. Slowly he turned from the workbench and faced the door. It had been locked—how could it have been opened so silently? There were two men standing beside it, motionless, watching him. Hans felt his heart trying to climb into his gullet, and summoned up what courage he could to challenge them. At least, he felt thankfully, he had little money here. Then he wondered if, after all, this was a good thing. They might be annoyed. . . .

"Who are you?" he asked. "What are you doing here?"

One of the men moved toward him while the other remained watching alertly from the door. They were both wearing very new overcoats, with hats low down on their heads so that Hans could not see their faces. They were too well dressed, he decided, to be ordinary holdup men.

"There's no need to be alarmed, Mr. Muller," replied the nearer man, reading his thoughts without difficulty. "This isn't a holdup. It's official. We're from—Security."

"I don't understand."

The other reached into a portfolio he had been carrying beneath his coat, and pulled out a sheaf of photographs. He riffled through them until he had found the one he wanted.

"You've given us quite a headache, Mr. Muller. It's taken us two weeks to find you—your employers were so secretive. No doubt they were anxious to hide you from their rivals. However, here we are and I'd like you to answer some questions."

"I'm not a spy!" answered Hans indignantly as the meaning of the words penetrated. "You can't do this! I'm a loyal American citizen!"

The other ignored the outburst. He handed over the photograph.

"Do you recognize this?" he said.

"Yes. It's the inside of Captain Zipp's spaceship."

"And you designed it?"

"Yes."

Another photograph came out of the file.

"And what about this?"

"That's the Martian city of Paldar, as seen from the air."

"Your own idea?"

"Certainly," Hans replied, now too indignant to be cautious.

"And *this*?"

"Oh, the proton gun. I was quite proud of that."

"Tell me, Mr. Muller—are these all your own ideas?"

"Yes, *I* don't steal from other people."

His questioner turned to his companion and spoke for a few minutes in a voice too low for Hans to hear. They seemed to reach agreement on some point, and the conference was over before Hans could make his intended grab at the telephone.

"I'm sorry," continued the intruder. "But there has been a serious leak. It may be—uh—accidental, even unconscious, but that does not affect the issue. We will have to investigate you. Please come with us."

There was such power and authority in the stranger's voice that Hans began to climb into his overcoat without a murmur. Somehow, he no longer doubted his visitors' credentials and never thought of asking for any proof. He was worried, but not yet seriously alarmed. Of course, it was obvious what had happened. He remembered hearing about a science-fiction writer during the war who had described the atom bomb with disconcerting accuracy. When so much secret research was going on, such accidents were bound to occur. He wondered just what it was he had given away.

At the doorway, he looked back into his workshop and at the men who were following him.

"It's all a ridiculous mistake," he said. "If I *did* show anything secret in the program, it was just a coincidence. I've never done anything to annoy the FBI."

It was then that the second man spoke at last, in very bad English and with a most peculiar accent.

"What is the FBI?" he asked.

But Hans didn't hear him. He had just seen the spaceship.

## NO MORNING AFTER

"BUT THIS IS TERRIBLE!" said the Supreme Scientist. "Surely there is *something* we can do!"

"Yes, Your Cognizance, but it will be extremely difficult. The planet is more than five hundred light-years away, and it is very hard to maintain contact. However, we believe we can establish a bridgehead. Unfortunately, that is not the only problem. So far, we have been quite unable to communicate with these beings. Their telepathic powers are exceedingly rudimentary—perhaps even nonexistent. And if we cannot talk to them, there is no way in which we can help."

There was a long mental silence while the Supreme Scientist analyzed the situation and arrived, as he always did, at the correct answer.

"Any intelligent race must have *some* telepathic individuals," he mused. "We must send out hundreds of observers, tuned to catch the first hint of stray thought. When you find a single responsive mind, concentrate all your efforts upon it. We *must* get our message through."

"Very good, Your Cognizance. It shall be done."

Across the abyss, across the gulf which light itself took half a thousand years to span, the questing intellects of the planet Thaar sent out their tendrils of thought, searching desperately for a single human being whose mind could perceive their presence. And as luck would have it, they encountered William Cross.

At least, they thought it was luck at the time, though later they were not so sure. In any case, they had little choice.

The combination of circumstances that opened Bill's mind to them lasted only for seconds, and was not likely to occur again this side of eternity.

There were three ingredients in the miracle: it is hard to say if one was more important than another. The first was the accident of position. A flask of water, when sunlight falls upon it, can act as a crude lens, concentrating the light into a small area. On an immeasurably larger scale, the dense core of the Earth was converging the waves that came from Thaar. In the ordinary way, the radiations of thought are unaffected by matter—they pass through it as effortlessly as light through glass. But there is rather a lot of matter in a planet, and the whole Earth was acting as a gigantic lens. As it turned, it was carrying Bill through its focus, where the feeble thought impulses from Thaar were concentrated a hundredfold.

Yet millions of other men were equally well placed: they received no message. But they were not rocket engineers: they had not spent years thinking and dreaming of space until it had become part of their very being.

And they were not, as Bill was, blind drunk, teetering on the last knife-edge of consciousness, trying to escape from reality into the world of dreams, where there were no disappointments and setbacks.

Of course, he could see the Army's point of view. "You are paid, Dr. Cross," General Potter had pointed out with unnecessary emphasis, "to design missiles, *not*—ah—spaceships. What you do in your spare time is your own concern, but I must ask you not to use the facilities of the establishment for your hobby. From now on, all projects for the computing section will have to be cleared by me. That is all."

They couldn't sack him, of course: he was too important. But he was not sure that he wanted to stay. He was not really sure of anything except that the job had backfired on him, and that Brenda had finally gone off with Johnny Gardner—putting events in their order of importance.

Wavering slightly, Bill cupped his chin in his hands and stared at the whitewashed brick wall on the other side of the table. The only attempt at ornamentation was a calendar from Lockheed and a glossy six-by-eight from Aerojet showing L'il Abner Mark I making a boosted take-off. Bill gazed morosely at a spot midway between the two pictures, and emptied his mind of thought. The barriers went down. . . .

At that moment, the massed intellects of Thaar gave a soundless cry of triumph, and the wall in front of Bill slowly dissolved into a swirling mist. He appeared to be looking down a tunnel that stretched to infinity. As a matter of fact, he was.

Bill studied the phenomenon with mild interest. It had a certain novelty, but was not up to the standard of previous hallucinations. And when the voice started to speak in his mind, he let it ramble on for some time before he did anything about it. Even when drunk, he had an old-fashioned prejudice against starting conversations with himself.

"Bill," the voice began, "listen carefully. We have had great difficulty in contacting you, and this is extremely important."

Bill doubted this on general principles. *Nothing* was important any more.

"We are speaking to you from a very distant planet," continued the voice in a tone of urgent friendliness. "You are the only human being we have been able to contact, so you *must* understand what we are saying."

Bill felt mildly worried, though in an impersonal sort of way, since it was now rather hard to focus on his own problems. How serious was it, he wondered, when you started to hear voices? Well, it was best not to get excited. You can take it or leave it, Dr. Cross, he told himself. Let's take it until it gets to be a nuisance.

"O.K.," he answered with bored indifference. "Go right ahead and talk to me. I won't mind as long as it's interesting."

There was a pause. Then the voice continued, in a slightly worried fashion.

"We don't quite understand. Our message isn't merely *interesting*. It's vital to your entire race, and you must notify your government immediately."

"I'm waiting," said Bill. "It helps to pass the time."

Five hundred light-years away, the Thaarns conferred hastily among themselves. Something seemed to be wrong, but they could not decide precisely what. There was no doubt that they had established contact, yet this was not the sort of reaction they had expected. Well, they could only proceed and hope for the best.

"Listen, Bill," they continued. "Our scientists have just discovered that your sun is about to explode. It will happen three days from now—seventy-four hours, to be exact. Nothing can stop it. But there's no need to be alarmed. We can save you, if you'll do what we say."

"Go on," said Bill. This hallucination was ingenious.

"We can create what we call a bridge—it's a kind of tunnel through space, like the one you're looking into now. The theory is far too complicated to explain, even to one of your mathematicians."

"Hold on a minute!" protested Bill. "I *am* a mathematician, and a darn good one, even when I'm sober. And I've read all about this kind of thing in the science-fiction magazines. I presume you're talking about some kind of short cut through a higher dimension of space. That's old stuff—pre-Einstein."

A sensation of distinct surprise seeped into Bill's mind. "We had no idea you were so advanced scientifically," said the Thaarns. "But we haven't time to talk about the theory. All that matters is this—if you were to step into that opening in front of you, you'd find yourself instantly on another planet. It's a short cut, as you said—in this case through the thirty-seventh dimension."

"And it leads to your world?"

"Oh no—you couldn't live here. But there are plenty of planets like Earth in the universe, and we've found one that will suit you. We'll establish bridgeheads like this all over Earth, so your people will only have to walk through them to be saved. Of course, they'll have to start building up civilization again when they reach their new homes, but it's their only hope. You have to pass on this message, and tell them what to do."

"I can just see them listening to me," said Bill. "Why don't you go and talk to the president?"

"Because yours was the only mind we were able to contact. Others seemed closed to us: we don't understand why."

"I could tell you," said Bill, looking at the nearly empty bottle in front of him. He was certainly getting his money's worth. What a remarkable thing the human mind was! Of course, there was nothing at all original in this dialogue: it was easy to see where the ideas came from. Only last week he'd been reading a story about the end of the world, and all this wishful thinking about bridges and tunnels through space was pretty obvious compensation for anyone who'd spent five years wrestling with recalcitrant rockets.

"If the sun does blow up," Bill asked abruptly—trying to catch his hallucination unawares—"what would happen?"

"Why, your planet would be melted instantly. All the planets, in fact, right out to Jupiter."

Bill had to admit that this was quite a grandiose conception. He let his mind play with the thought, and the more he considered it, the more he liked it.

"My dear hallucination," he remarked pityingly, "if I believed you, d'you know what I'd say?"

"But you *must* believe us!" came the despairing cry across the light-years.

Bill ignored it. He was warming to his theme.

"I'd tell you this. *It would be the best thing that could possibly happen.* Yes, it would save a whole lot of misery. No one would have to worry about the Russians and the atom bomb and the high cost of living. Oh, it would be wonderful! It's just what everybody really wants. Nice of you to come along and tell us, but just you go back home and pull your old bridge after you."

There was consternation on Thaar. The Supreme Scientist's brain, floating like a great mass of coral in its tank of nutrient solution, turned slightly yellow about the edges—something it had not done since the Xantil invasion, five thousand years ago. At least fifteen psychologists had nervous breakdowns and were never the same again. The main computer in the College of Cosmophysics started dividing every number in its memory circuits by zero, and promptly blew all its fuses.

And on Earth, Bill Cross was really hitting his stride.

"Look at *me*," he said, pointing a wavering finger at his chest. "I've spent years trying to make rockets do something useful, and they tell me I'm only allowed to build guided missiles, so that we can all blow each other up. The sun will make a neater job of it, and if you did give us another planet we'd only start the whole damn thing all over again."

He paused sadly, marshaling his morbid thoughts.

"And now Brenda heads out of town without even leaving a note. So you'll pardon my lack of enthusiasm for your Boy Scout act."

He couldn't have said "enthusiasm" aloud, Bill realized. But he could still think it, which was an interesting scientific discovery. As he got drunker and drunker, would his cogitation—whoops, *that* nearly threw him!—finally drop down to words of one syllable?

In a final despairing exertion, the Thaarns sent their thoughts along the tunnel between the stars.

"You can't really mean it, Bill! Are *all* human beings like you?"

Now that was an interesting philosophical question! Bill considered it carefully—or as carefully as he could in view of the warm, rosy glow that was now beginning to envelop him. After all, things might be worse. He could get another job, if only for the pleasure of telling General Porter what he could do with his three stars. And as for Brenda—well, women were like streetcars: there'd always be another along in a minute.

Best of all, there was a second bottle of whisky in the Top Secret file. Oh, frabjous day! He rose unsteadily to his feet and wavered across the room.

For the last time, Thaar spoke to Earth.

"Bill!" it repeated desperately. "Surely all human beings can't be like you!"

Bill turned and looked into the swirling tunnel. Strange— it seemed to be lighted with flecks of starlight, and was really rather pretty. He felt proud of himself: not many people could imagine *that*.

"Like me?" he said. "No, they're not." He smiled smugly across the light-years, as the rising tide of euphoria lifted him out of his despondency. "Come to think of it," he added, "there are a lot of people much worse off than me. Yes, I guess I must be one of the lucky ones, after all."

He blinked in mild surprise, for the tunnel had suddenly collapsed upon itself and the whitewashed wall was there again, exactly as it had always been. Thaar knew when it was beaten.

"So much for *that* hallucination," thought Bill. "I was getting tired of it, anyway. Let's see what the next one's like."

As it happened, there wasn't a next one, for five seconds later he passed out cold, just as he was setting the combination of the file cabinet.

The next two days were rather vague and bloodshot, and he forgot all about the interview.

On the third day something was nagging at the back of his mind: he might have remembered if Brenda hadn't turned up again and kept him busy being forgiving.

And there wasn't a fourth day, of course.

## VENTURE TO THE MOON

### The Starting Line

THE STORY OF the first lunar expedition has been written so many times that some people will doubt if there is anything fresh to be said about it. Yet all the official reports and eyewitness accounts, the on-the-spot recordings and broadcasts never, in my opinion, gave the full picture. They said a great deal about the discoveries that were made—but very little about the men who made them.

As captain of the *Endeavour* and thus commander of the British party, I was able to observe a good many things you will not find in the history books, and some—though not all—of them can now be told. One day, I hope, my opposite numbers on the *Goddard* and the *Ziolkovski* will give their points of view. But as Commander Vandenburg is still on Mars and Commander Krasnin is somewhere inside the orbit of Venus, it looks as if we will have to wait a few more years for *their* memoirs.

Confession, it is said, is good for the soul. I shall certainly feel much happier when I have told the true story behind the timing of the first lunar flight, about which there has always been a good deal of mystery.

As everyone knows, the American, Russian, and British ships were assembled in the orbit of Space Station Three, five hundred miles above the Earth, from components flown up by relays of freight rockets. Though all the parts had been prefabricated, the assembly and testing of the ships took over two years, by which time a great many people—who did not realize the complexity of the task—were beginning to get slightly impatient. They had seen dozens of photos and telecasts of the three ships floating there in space beside Station Three, apparently quite complete and ready to pull away from Earth at a moment's notice. What the pictures didn't show was the careful and tedious work still in progress as thousands of pipes, wires, motors, and instruments were fitted and subjected to every conceivable test.

There was no definite target date for departure; since the moon is always at approximately the same distance, you can leave for it at almost any time you like—once you are ready. It makes practically no difference, from the point of view of fuel consumption, if you blast off at full moon or new moon or at any time in between. We were very careful to make no predictions about blast-off, though everyone was always trying to get us to fix the time. So many things can go wrong in a spaceship, and we were not going to say good-by to Earth until we were ready down to the last detail.

I shall always remember the last commanders' conference, aboard the space station, when we all announced that we were ready. Since it was a co-operative venture, each party specializing in some particular task, it had been agreed that we should all make our landings within the same twenty-four-hour period, on the preselected site in the Mare Imbrium. The details of the journey, however, had been left to the individual commanders, presumably in the hope that we would not copy each other's mistakes.

"I'll be ready," said Commander Vandenburg, "to make my first dummy take-off at 0900 tomorrow. What about you, gentlemen? Shall we ask Earth Control to stand by for all three of us?"

"That's O.K. by me," said Krasnin, who could never be convinced that his American slang was twenty years out of date.

I nodded my agreement. It was true that one bank of fuel gauges was still misbehaving, but that didn't really matter; they would be fixed by the time the tanks were filled.

The dummy run consisted of an exact replica of a real blast-off, with everyone carrying out the job he would do when the time came for the genuine thing. We had practiced, of course, in mock-ups down on Earth, but this was a perfect imitation of what would happen to us when we finally took off for the moon. All that was missing was the roar of the motors that would tell us that the voyage had begun.

We did six complete imitations of blast-off, took the ships to pieces to eliminate anything that hadn't behaved perfectly, then did six more. The *Endeavour*, the *Goddard*, and the *Ziolkovski* were all in the same state of serviceability. There now only remained the job of fueling up, and we would be ready to leave.

The suspense of those last few hours is not something I would care to go through again. The eyes of the world were upon us; departure time had now been set, with an uncertainty of only a few hours. All the final tests had been made, and we were convinced that our ships were as ready as humanly possible.

It was then that I had an urgent and secret personal radio call from a very high official indeed, and a suggestion was made which had so much authority behind it that there was little point in pretending that it wasn't an order. The first flight to the moon, I was reminded, was a co-operative venture—but think of the prestige if *we* got there first. It need only be by a couple of hours. . . .

I was shocked at the suggestion, and said so. By this time Vandenburg and Krasnin were good friends of mine, and we were all in this together. I made every excuse I could and said that since our flight paths had already been computed there wasn't anything that could be done about it. Each ship was making the journey by the most economical route, to conserve fuel. If we started together, we should arrive together —within seconds.

Unfortunately, someone had thought of the answer to that. Our three ships, fueled up and with their crews standing by, would be circling Earth in a state of complete readiness for several hours before they actually pulled away from their satellite orbits and headed out to the moon. At our five-hundred-mile altitude, we took ninety-five minutes to make one circuit of the Earth, and only once every revolution would the moment be ripe to begin the voyage. If we could jump the gun by one revolution, the others would have to wait that ninety-five minutes before they could follow. And so they would land on the moon ninety-five minutes behind us.. . . .

I won't go into the arguments, and I'm still a little ashamed that I yielded and agreed to deceive my two colleagues. We were in the shadow of Earth, in momentary eclipse, when the carefully calculated moment came. Vandenburg and Krasnin, honest fellows, thought I was going to make one more round trip with them before we all set off together. I have seldom felt a bigger heel in my life than when I pressed the firing key and felt the sudden thrust of the motors as they swept me away from my mother world.

For the next ten minutes we had no time for anything but our instruments, as we checked to see that the *Endeavour* was forging ahead along her precomputed orbit. Almost at the moment that we finally escaped from Earth and could cut the motors, we burst out of shadow into the full blaze of the sun. There would be no more night until we reached the moon, after five days of effortless and silent coasting through space.

Already Space Station Three and the two other ships must be a thousand miles behind. In eighty-five more minutes Vandenburg and Krasnin would be back at the correct starting point and could take off after me, as we had all planned. But they could never overcome my lead, and I hoped they wouldn't be too mad at me when we met again on the moon.

I switched on the rear camera and looked back at the distant gleam of the space station, just emerging from the shadow of Earth. It was some moments before I realized that the *Goddard* and the *Ziolkovski* weren't still floating beside it where I'd left them. . . .

No; they were just half a mile away, neatly matching my velocity. I stared at them in utter disbelief for a second, before I realized that every one of us had had the same idea. "Why, you pair of double-crossers!" I gasped. Then I began to laugh so much that it was several minutes before I dared call up a very worried Earth Control and tell them that everything had gone according to plan—though in no case was it the plan that had been originally announced. . . .

We were all very sheepish when we radioed each other to exchange mutual congratulations. Yet at the same time, I think everyone was secretly pleased that it had turned out this way. For the rest of the trip, we were never more than a few miles apart, and the actual landing maneuvers were so well synchronized that our three braking jets hit the moon simultaneously.

Well, almost simultaneously. I might make something of the fact that the recorder tape shows I touched down two-fifths of a second ahead of Krasnin. But I'd better not, for Vandenburg was precisely the same amount ahead of me.

On a quarter-of-a-million-mile trip, I think you could call that a photo finish. . . .

## Robin Hood, F.R.S.

WE HAD LANDED early in the dawn of the long lunar day, and the slanting shadows lay all around us, extending for miles across the plain. They would slowly shorten as the sun rose higher in the sky, until at noon they would almost vanish—but noon was still five days away, as we measured time on Earth, and nightfall was seven days later still. We had almost two weeks of daylight ahead of us before the sun set and the bluely gleaming Earth became the mistress of the sky.

There was little time for exploration during those first hectic days. We had to unload the ships, grow accustomed to the alien conditions surrounding us, learn to handle our electrically powered tractors and scooters, and erect the igloos that would serve as homes, offices, and labs until the time came to leave. At a pinch, we could live in the spaceships, but it would be excessively uncomfortable and cramped. The igloos were not exactly commodious, but they were luxury after five days in space. Made of tough, flexible plastic, they were blown up like balloons, and their interiors were then partitioned into separate rooms. Air locks allowed access to the outer world, and a good deal of plumbing linked to the ships' air-purification plants kept the atmosphere breathable. Needless to say, the American igloo was the biggest one, and had come complete with everything, *including* the kitchen sink—not to

mention a washing machine, which we and the Russians were
always borrowing.

It was late in the "afternoon"—about ten days after we
had landed—before we were properly organized and could
think about serious scientific work. The first parties made
nervous little forays out into the wilderness around the base,
familiarizing themselves with the territory. Of course, we
already possessed minutely detailed maps and photographs of
the region in which we had landed, but it was surprising how
misleading they could sometimes be. What had been marked
as a small hill on a chart often looked like a mountain to a
man toiling along in a space suit, and apparently smooth
plains were often covered knee-deep with dust, which made
progress extremely slow and tedious.

These were minor difficulties, however, and the low gravity
—which gave all objects only a sixth of their terrestrial
weight—compensated for much. As the scientists began to
accumulate their results and specimens, the radio and TV
circuits with Earth became busier and busier, until they were
in continuous operation. We were taking no chances; even
if *we* didn't get home, the knowledge we were gathering
would do so.

The first of the automatic supply rockets landed two days
before sunset, precisely according to plan. We saw its braking
jets flame briefly against the stars, then blast again a few
seconds before touchdown. The actual landing was hidden
from us, since for safety reasons the dropping ground was
three miles from the base. And on the moon, three miles is
well over the curve of the horizon.

When we got to the robot, it was standing slightly askew
on its tripod shock absorbers, but in perfect condition. So
was everything aboard it, from instruments to food. We
carried the stores back to base in triumph, and had a celebra-
tion that was really rather overdue. The men had been working too hard, and could do with some relaxation.

It was quite a party; the high light, I think, was Commander Krasnin trying to do a Cossack dance in a space suit.
Then we turned our minds to competitive sports, but found
that, for obvious reasons, outdoor activities were somewhat
restricted. Games like croquet or bowls would have been
practical had we had the equipment; but cricket and football
were definitely out. In that gravity, even a football would go
half a mile if it were given a good kick—and a cricket ball
would never be seen again.

Professor Trevor Williams was the first person to think of
a practical lunar sport. He was our astronomer, and also one

of the youngest men ever to be made a Fellow of the Royal Society, being only thirty when this ultimate accolade was conferred upon him. His work on methods of interplanetary navigation had made him world famous; less well known, however, was his skill as a toxophilite. For two years in succession he had been archery champion for Wales. I was not surprised, therefore, when I discovered him shooting at a target propped up on a pile of lunar slag.

The bow was a curious one, strung with steel control wire and shaped from a laminated plastic bar. I wondered where Trevor had got hold of it, then remembered that the robot freight rocket had now been cannibalized and bits of it were appearing in all sorts of unexpected places. The arrows, however, were the really interesting feature. To give them stability on the airless moon, where, of course, feathers would be useless, Trevor had managed to rifle them. There was a little gadget on the bow that set them spinning, like bullets, when they were fired, so that they kept on course when they left the bow.

Even with this rather makeshift equipment, it was possible to shoot a mile if one wished to. However, Trevor didn't want to waste arrows, which were not easy to make; he was more interested in seeing the sort of accuracy he could get. It was uncanny to watch the almost flat trajectory of the arrows: they seemed to be traveling parallel with the ground. If he wasn't careful, someone warned Trevor, his arrows might become lunar satellites and would hit him in the back when they completed their orbit.

The second supply rocket arrived the next day, but this time things didn't go according to plan. It made a perfect touchdown, but unfortunately the radar-controlled automatic pilot made one of those mistakes that such simple-minded machines delight in doing. It spotted the only really unclimbable hill in the neighborhood, locked its beam onto the summit of it, and settled down there like an eagle descending upon its mountain aerie.

Our badly needed supplies were five hundred feet above our heads, and in a few hours night would be falling. What was to be done?

About fifteen people made the same suggestion at once, and for the next few minutes there was a great scurrying about as we rounded up all the nylon line on the base. Soon there was more than a thousand yards of it coiled in neat loops at Trevor's feet while we all waited expectantly. He tied one end to his arrow, drew the bow, and aimed it experimentally straight toward the stars. The arrow rose a little more than half the height of the cliff; then the weight of the line pulled it back.

"Sorry," said Trevor. "I just can't make it. And don't forget—we'd have to send up some kind of grapnel as well, if we want the end to stay up there."

There was much gloom for the next few minutes, as we watched the coils of line fall slowly back from the sky. The situation was really somewhat absurd. In our ships we had enough energy to carry us a quarter of a million miles from the moon—yet we were baffled by a puny little cliff. If we had time, we could probably find a way up to the top from the other side of the hill, but that would mean traveling several miles. It would be dangerous, and might well be impossible, during the few hours of daylight that were left.

Scientists were never baffled for long, and too many ingenious (sometimes overingenious) minds were working on the problem for it to remain unresolved. But this time it was a little more difficult, and only three people got the answer simultaneously. Trevor thought it over, then said noncommittally, "Well, it's worth trying."

The preparations took a little while, and we were all watching anxiously as the rays of the sinking sun crept higher and higher up the sheer cliff looming above us. Even if Trevor could get a line and grapnel up there, I thought to myself, it would not be easy making the ascent while encumbered with a space suit. I have no head for heights, and was glad that several mountaineering enthusiasts had already volunteered for the job.

At last everything was ready. The line had been carefully arranged so that it would lift from the ground with the minimum of hindrance. A light grapnel had been attached to the line a few feet behind the arrow; we hoped that it would catch in the rocks up there and wouldn't let us down—all too literally—when we put our trust in it.

This time, however, Trevor was not using a single arrow. He attached four to the line, at two-hundred-yard intervals. And I shall never forget that incongruous spectacle of the space-suited figure, gleaming in the last rays of the setting sun, as it drew its bow against the sky.

The arrow sped toward the stars, and before it had lifted more than fifty feet Trevor was already fitting the second one to his improvised bow. It raced after its predecessor, carrying the other end of the long loop that was now being hoisted into space. Almost at once the third followed, lifting its section of line—and I swear that the fourth arrow, with its section, was on the way before the first had noticeably slackened its momentum.

Now that there was no question of a single arrow lifting the entire length of line, it was not hard to reach the required altitude. The first two times the grapnel fell back; then it caught firmly somewhere up on the hidden plateau—and the first volunteer began to haul himself up the line. It was true that he weighed only about thirty pounds in this low gravity, but it was still a long way to fall.

He didn't. The stores in the freight rocket started coming down the cliff within the next hour, and everything essential had been lowered before nightfall. I must confess, however, that my satisfaction was considerably abated when one of the engineers proudly showed me the mouth organ he had sent from Earth. Even then I felt certain that we would all be very tired of that instrument before the long lunar night had ended. . . .

But that, of course, was hardly Trevor's fault. As we walked back to the ship together, through the great pools of shadow that were flowing swiftly over the plain, he made a proposal that, I am sure, has puzzled thousands of people ever since the detailed maps of the first lunar expedition were published.

After all, it does seem a little odd that a flat and lifeless plain, broken by a single small mountain, should now be labeled on all the charts of the moon as Sherwood Forest.

## Green Fingers

I AM VERY sorry, now that it's too late, that I never got to know Vladimir Surov. As I remember him, he was a quiet little man who could understand English but couldn't speak it well enough to make conversation. Even to his colleagues, I suspect he was a bit of an enigma. Whenever I went aboard the *Ziolkovski,* he would be sitting in a corner working on his notes or peering through a microscope, a man who clung to his privacy even in the tight and tiny world of a spaceship. The rest of the crew did not seem to mind his aloofness; when they spoke to him, it was clear that they regarded him with tolerant affection, as well as with respect. That was hardly surprising; the work he had done developing plants and trees that could flourish far inside the Arctic Circle had already made him the most famous botanist in Russia.

The fact that the Russian expedition had taken a botanist to the moon had caused a good deal of amusement, though it was really no odder than the fact that there were biologists on both the British and American ships. During the years before the first lunar landing, a good deal of evidence had accumulated hinting that some form of vegetation might exist on the moon, despite its airlessness and lack of water. The president of the U.S.S.R. Academy of Science was one of the leading proponents of this theory, and being too old to make the trip himself had done the next best thing by sending Surov.

The complete absence of any such vegetation, living or fossil, in the thousand or so square miles explored by our various parties was the first big disappointment the moon had reserved for us. Even those skeptics who were quite certain that no form of life could exist on the moon would have been very glad to have been proved wrong—as of course they were, five years later, when Richards and Shannon made their astonishing discovery inside the great walled plain of Eratosthenes. But *that* revelation still lay in the future; at the time of the first landing, it seemed that Surov had come to the moon in vain.

He did not appear unduly depressed, but kept himself as busy as the rest of the crew studying soil samples and looking after the little hydroponic farm whose pressurized, transparent tubes formed a gleaming network around the *Ziolkovski*. Neither we nor the Americans had gone in for this sort of thing, having calculated that it was better to ship food from Earth than to grow it on the spot—at least until the time came to set up a permanent base. We were right in terms of economics, but wrong in terms of morale. The tiny airtight greenhouses inside which Surov grew his vegetables and dwarf fruit trees were an oasis upon which we often feasted our eyes when we had grown tired of the immense desolation surrounding us.

One of the many disadvantages of being commander was that I seldom had much chance to do any active exploring; I was too busy preparing reports for Earth, checking stores, arranging programs and duty rosters, conferring with my opposite numbers in the American and Russian ships, and trying—not always successfully—to guess what would go wrong next. As a result, I sometimes did not go outside the base for two or three days at a time, and it was a standing joke that my space suit was a haven for moths.

Perhaps it is because of this that I can remember all my trips outside so vividly; certainly I can recall my only encounter with Surov. It was near noon, with the sun high above the southern mountains and the new Earth a barely visible thread of silver a few degrees away from it. Henderson, our geophysicist, wanted to take some magnetic readings at a series of check points a couple of miles to the east of the base. Everyone else was busy, and I was momentarily on top of my work, so we set off together on foot.

The journey was not long enough to merit taking one of the scooters, especially because the charges in the batteries were getting low. In any case, I always enjoyed walking out in the open on the moon. It was not merely the scenery, which even at its most awe-inspiring one can grow accustomed to after a while. No—what I never tired of was the effortless, slow-motion way in which every step took me bounding over the landscape, giving me the freedom that before the coming of space flight men only knew in dreams.

We had done the job and were halfway home when I noticed a figure moving across the plain about a mile to the south of us—not far, in fact, from the Russian base. I snapped my field glasses down inside my helmet and took a careful look at the other explorer. Even at close range, of course, you can't identify a man in a space suit, but because the suits are always coded by color and number that makes no practical difference.

"Who is it?" asked Henderson over the short-range radio channel to which we were both tuned.

"Blue suit, Number 3—that would be Surov. But I don't understand. *He's by himself.*"

It is one of the most fundamental rules of lunar exploration that no one goes anywhere alone on the surface of the moon. So many accidents can happen, which would be trivial if you were with a companion—but fatal if you were by yourself. How would you manage, for example, if your space suit developed a slow leak in the small of the back and you couldn't put on a repair patch? That may sound funny; but it's happened.

"Perhaps his buddy has had an accident and he's going to fetch help," suggested Henderson. "Maybe we had better call him."

I shook my head. Surov was obviously in no hurry. He had been out on a trip of his own, and was making his leisurely way back to the *Ziolkovski*. It was no concern of mine if Commander Krasnin let his people go out on solo trips, though it seemed a deplorable practice. And if Surov was breaking regulations, it was equally no concern of mine to report him.

During the next two months, my men often spotted Surov making his lone way over the landscape, but he always avoided them if they got too near. I made some discreet inquiries, and found that Commander Krasnin had been forced, owing to shortage of men, to relax some of his safety rules. But I couldn't find out what Surov was up to, though I never dreamed that his commander was equally in the dark.

It was with an "I told you so" feeling that I got Krasnin's emergency call. We had all had men in trouble before and had had to send out help, but this was the first time anyone had been lost and had not replied when his ship had sent out the recall signal. There was a hasty radio conference, a line of action was drawn up, and search parties fanned out from each of the three ships.

Once again I was with Henderson, and it was only common sense for us to backtrack along the route that we had seen Surov following. It was in what we regarded as "our" territory, quite some distance away from Surov's own ship, and as we scrambled up the low foothills it occurred to me for the first time that the Russian might have been doing something he wanted to keep from his colleagues. What it might be, I could not imagine.

Henderson found him, and yelled for help over his suit radio. But it was much too late; Surov was lying, face down, his deflated suit crumpled around him. He had been kneeling when something had smashed the plastic globe of his helmet; you could see how he had pitched forward and died instantaneously.

When Commander Krasnin reached us, we were still staring at the unbelievable object that Surov had been examining when he died. It was about three feet high, a leathery, greenish oval rooted to the rocks with a widespread network of tendrils. Yes—rooted; for it was a plant. A few yards away were two others, much smaller and apparently dead, since they were blackened and withered.

My first reaction was: "So there *is* life on the moon, after all!" It was not until Krasnin's voice spoke in my ears that I realized how much more marvelous was the truth.

"Poor Vladimir!" he said. "We knew he was a genius, yet we laughed at him when he told us of his dream. So he kept his greatest work a secret. He conquered the Arctic with his hybrid wheat, but *that* was only a beginning. He has brought life to the moon—and death as well."

As I stood there, in that first moment of astonished revelation, it still seemed a miracle. Today, all the world knows the history of "Surov's cactus," as it was inevitably if quite inaccurately christened, and it has lost much of its wonder. His notes have told the full story, and have described the years of experimentation that finally led him to a plant whose leathery skin would enable it to survive in vacuum, and whose far-ranging, acid-secreting roots would enable it to grow upon rocks where even lichens would be hard put to thrive. And we have seen the realization of the second stage of Surov's dream, for the cactus which will forever bear his name has already broken up vast areas of the lunar rock and so prepared a way for the more specialized plants that now feed every human being upon the moon.

Krasnin bent down beside the body of his colleague and lifted it effortlessly against the low gravity. He fingered the shattered fragments of the plastic helmet, and shook his head in perplexity.

"What could have happened to him?" he said. "It almost looks as if the plant did it, but that's ridiculous."

The green enigma stood there on the no-longer barren plain, tantalizing us with its promise and its mystery. Then Henderson said slowly, as if thinking aloud:

"I believe I've got the answer; I've just remembered some of the botany I did at school. If Surov designed this plant for lunar conditions, how would he arrange for it to propagate itself? The seeds would have to be scattered over a very wide area in the hope of finding a few suitable places to grow. There are no birds or animals here to carry them, in the way that happens on Earth. I can only think of one solution—and some of our terrestrial plants have already used it."

He was interrupted by my yell. Something had hit with a resounding clang against the metal waistband of my suit. It did no damage, but it was so sudden and unexpected that it took me utterly by surprise.

A seed lay at my feet, about the size and shape of a plum stone. A few yards away, we found the one that had shattered Surov's helmet as he bent down. He must have known that the plant was ripe, but in his eagerness to examine it he had forgotten what that implied. I have seen a cactus throw its seed a quarter of a mile under the low lunar gravity. Surov had been shot at point-blank range by his own creation.

## All That Glitters

THIS IS REALLY Commander Vandenburg's story, but he is too many millions of miles away to tell it. It concerns his geophysicist, Dr. Paynter, who was generally believed to have gone to the moon to get away from his wife.

At one time or other, we were all supposed (often by our

wives) to have done just that. However, in Paynter's case, there was just enough truth to make it stick.

It was not that he disliked his wife; one could almost say the contrary. He would do anything for her, but unfortunately the things that she wanted him to do cost rather too much. She was a lady of extravagant tastes, and such ladies are advised not to marry scientists—even scientists who go to the moon.

Mrs. Paynter's weakness was for jewelry, particularly diamonds. As might be expected, this was a weakness that caused her husband a good deal of worry. Being a conscientious as well as an affectionate husband, he did not merely worry about it—he did something about it. He became one of the world's leading experts on diamonds, from the scientific rather than the commercial point of view, and probably knew more about their composition, origin, and properties than any other man alive. Unfortunately, you may know a lot about diamonds without ever possessing any, and her husband's erudition was not something that Mrs. Paynter could wear around her neck when she went to a party.

Geophysics, as I have mentioned, was Dr. Paynter's real business; diamonds were merely a side line. He had developed many remarkable surveying instruments which could probe the interior of the Earth by means of electric impulses and magnetic waves, so giving a kind of X-ray picture of the hidden strata far below. It was hardly surprising, therefore, that he was one of the men chosen to pry into the mysterious interior of the moon.

He was quite eager to go, but it seemed to Commander Vandenburg that he was reluctant to leave Earth at this particular moment. A number of men had shown such symptoms; sometimes they were due to fears that could not be eradicated, and an otherwise promising man had to be left behind. In Paynter's case, however, the reluctance was quite impersonal. He was in the middle of a big experiment—something he had been working on all his life—and he didn't want to leave Earth until it was finished. However, the first lunar expedition could not wait for him, so he had to leave his project in the hands of his assistants. He was continually exchanging cryptic radio messages with them, to the great annoyance of the signals section of Space Station Three.

In the wonder of a new world waiting to be explored, Paynter soon forgot his earthly preoccupations. He would dash hither and yon over the lunar landscape on one of the neat little electric scooters the Americans had brought with them, carrying seismographs, magnetometers, gravity meters, and all the other esoteric tools of the geophysicist's trade. He was trying to learn, in a few weeks, what it had taken men hundreds of years to discover about their own planet. It was true that he had only a small sample of the moon's fourteen million square miles of territory to explore, but he intended to make a thorough job of it.

From time to time he continued to get messages from his colleagues back on Earth, as well as brief but affectionate signals from Mrs. P. Neither seemed to interest him very much; even when you are not so busy that you hardly have time to sleep, a quarter of a million miles puts most of your personal affairs in a different perspective. I think that on the moon Dr. Paynter was really happy for the first time in his life; if so, he was not the only one.

Not far from our base there was a rather fine crater pit, a great blowhole in the lunar surface almost two miles from rim to rim. Though it was fairly close at hand, it was outside the normal area of our joint operations, and we had been on the moon for six weeks before Paynter led a party of three men off in one of the baby tractors to have a look at it. They disappeared from radio range over the edge of the moon, but we weren't worried about that because if they ran into trouble they could always call Earth and get any message relayed back to us.

Paynter and his men were gone forty-eight hours, which is about the maximum for continuous working on the moon, even with booster drugs. At first their little expedition was quite uneventful and therefore quite unexciting; everything went according to plan. They reached the crater, inflated their pressurized igloo and unpacked their stores, took their instrument readings, and then set up a portable drill to get core samples. It was while he was waiting for the drill to bring him up a nice section of the moon that Paynter made his second great discovery. He had made his first about ten hours before, but he didn't know it yet.

Around the lip of the crater, lying where they had been thrown up by the great explosions that had convulsed the lunar landscape three hundred million years before, were immense piles of rock which must have come from many miles down in the moon's interior. Anything he could do with his little drill, thought Paynter, could hardly compare with *this*. Unfortunately, the mountain-sized geological specimens that lay all around him were not neatly arranged in their correct order; they had been scattered over the landscape, much farther than the eye could see, according to the arbitrary violence of the eruptions that had blasted them into space.

Paynter climbed over these immense slag heaps, taking a swing at likely samples with his little hammer. Presently his colleagues heard him yell, and saw him come running back to them carrying what appeared to be a lump of rather poor quality glass. It was some time before he was sufficiently coherent to explain what all the fuss was about—and some time later still before the expedition remembered its real job and got back to work.

Vandenburg watched the returning party as it headed back to the ship. The four men didn't seem as tired as one would have expected, considering the fact that they had been on their feet for two days. Indeed, there was a certain jauntiness about their movements which even the space suits couldn't wholly conceal. You could see that the expedition had been a success. In that case, Paynter would have two causes for congratulation. The priority message that had just come from Earth was very cryptic, but it was clear that Paynter's work there—whatever it was—had finally reached a triumphant conclusion.

Commander Vandenburg almost forgot the message when he saw what Paynter was holding in his hand. He knew what a raw diamond looked like, and this was the second largest that anyone had ever seen. Only the Cullinan, tipping the scales at 3,026 carats, beat it by a slender margin. "We ought to have expected it," he heard Paynter babble happily. "Diamonds are always found associated with volcanic vents. But somehow I never thought the analogy would hold here."

Vandenburg suddenly remembered the signal, and handed it over to Paynter. He read it quickly, and his jaw dropped. Never in his life, Vandenburg told me, had he seen a man so instantly deflated by a message of congratulation. The signal read: WE'VE DONE IT. TEST 541 WITH MODIFIED PRESSURE CONTAINER COMPLETE SUCCESS. NO PRACTICAL LIMIT TO SIZE. COSTS NEGLIGIBLE.

"What's the matter?" said Vandenburg, when he saw the stricken look on Paynter's face. "It doesn't seem bad news to me, whatever it means."

Paynter gulped two or three times like a stranded fish, then stared helplessly at the great crystal that almost filled the palm of his hand. He tossed it into the air, and it floated back in that slow-motion way everything has under lunar gravity.

Finally he found his voice.

"My lab's been working for years," he said, "trying to synthesize diamonds. Yesterday this thing was worth a million dollars. Today it's worth a couple of hundred. I'm not sure I'll bother to carry it back to Earth."

Well, he *did* carry it back; it seemed a pity not to. For about three months, Mrs. P. had the finest diamond necklace in the world, worth every bit of a thousand dollars— mostly the cost of cutting and polishing. Then the Paynter Process went into commercial production, and a month later she got her divorce. The grounds were extreme mental cruelty; and I suppose you could say it was justified.

## Watch This Space

IT WAS QUITE a surprise to discover, when I looked it up, that the most famous experiment we carried out while we were on the moon had its beginnings way back in 1955. At that time, high-altitude rocket research had been going for only about ten years, mostly at White Sands, New Mexico. Nineteen fifty-five was the date of one of the most spectacular of those early experiments, one that involved the ejection of sodium onto the upper atmosphere.

On Earth, even on the clearest night, the sky between the stars isn't completely dark. There's a very faint background glow, and part of it is caused by the fluorescence of sodium atoms a hundred miles up. Since it would take the sodium in a good many cubic miles of the upper atmosphere to fill a single matchbox, it seemed to the early investigators that they could make quite a fireworks display if they used a rocket to dump a few pounds of the stuff into the ionosphere.

They were right. The sodium squirted out of a rocket above White Sands early in 1955 produced a great yellow glow in the sky which was visible, like a kind of artificial moonlight, for over an hour, before the atoms dispersed. This experiment wasn't done for fun (though it *was* fun) but for a serious scientific purpose. Instruments trained on this glow were able to gather new knowledge about the upper air—knowledge that went into the stockpile of information without which space flight would never have been possible.

When they got to the moon, the Americans decided that it would be a good idea to repeat the experiment there, on a much larger scale. A few hundred kilograms of sodium fired up from the surface would produce a display that would be visible from Earth, with a good pair of field glasses, as it fluoresced its way up through the lunar atmosphere.

(Some people, by the way, still don't realize that the moon *has* an atmosphere. It's about a million times too thin to be breathable, but if you have the right instruments you can detect it. As a meteor shield, it's first-rate, for though it may be tenuous it's hundreds of miles deep.)

Everyone had been talking about the experiment for days. The sodium bomb had arrived from Earth in the last supply rocket, and a very impressive piece of equipment it looked. Its operation was extremely simple; when ignited, an incendiary charge vaporized the sodium until a high pressure was built up, then a diaphragm burst and the stuff was squirted up into the sky through a specially shaped nozzle. It would be shot off soon after nightfall, and when the cloud of sodium rose out of the moon's shadow into direct sunlight it would start to glow with tremendous brilliance.

Nightfall, on the moon, is one of the most awe-inspiring sights in the whole of nature, made doubly so because as you watch the sun's flaming disk creep so slowly below the mountains you know that it will be fourteen days before you see it again. But it does not bring darkness—at least, not on this side of the moon. There is always the Earth, hanging motionless in the sky, the one heavenly body that neither rises nor sets. The light pouring back from her clouds and seas floods the lunar landscape with a soft, blue-green radiance, so that it is often easier to find your way around at night than under the fierce glare of the sun.

Even those who were not supposed to be on duty had come out to watch the experiment. The sodium bomb had been placed at the middle of the big triangle formed by the three ships, and stood upright with its nozzles pointing at the stars. Dr. Anderson, the astronomer of the American team, was testing the firing circuits, but everyone else was at a respectful distance. The bomb looked perfectly capable of living up to its name, though it was really about as dangerous as a soda-water siphon.

All the optical equipment of the three expeditions seemed to have been gathered together to record the performance. Telescopes, spectroscopes, motion-picture cameras, and everything else one could think of were lined up ready for action. And this, I knew, was nothing compared with the battery that must be zeroed in on us from Earth. Every amateur astronomer who could see the moon tonight would be standing by in his back garden, listening to the radio commentary that told him of the progress of the experiment. I glanced up at the gleaming planet that dominated the sky above me; the land areas seemed to be fairly free from cloud, so the folks at home should have a good view. That seemed only fair; after all, they were footing the bill.

There were still fifteen minutes to go. Not for the first time, I wished there was a reliable way of smoking a cigarette inside a space suit without getting the helmet so badly fogged that you couldn't see. Our scientists had solved so many much more difficult problems; it seemed a pity that they couldn't do something about *that* one.

To pass the time—for this was an experiment where I had nothing to do—I switched on my suit radio and listened to Dave Bolton, who was making a very good job of the commentary. Dave was our chief navigator, and a brilliant mathematician. He also had a glib tongue and a picturesque turn of speech, and sometimes his recordings had to be censored by the B.B.C. There was nothing they could do about this one, however, for it was going out live from the relay stations on Earth.

Dave had finished a brief and lucid explanation of the purpose of the experiment, describing how the cloud of glowing sodium would enable us to analyze the lunar atmosphere as it rose through it at approximately a thousand miles an hour. "However," he went on to tell the waiting millions on Earth, "let's make one point clear. Even when the bomb has gone off, you won't see a darn thing for ten minutes—and neither will we. The sodium cloud will be completely invisible while it's rising up through the darkness of the moon's shadow. Then, quite suddenly, it will flash into brilliance as it enters the sun's rays, which are streaming past over our heads right now as we stare up into space. No one is quite sure how bright it will be, but it's a pretty safe guess that you'll be able to see it in any telescope bigger than a two-inch. So it should just be within the range of a good pair of binoculars."

He had to keep this sort of thing up for another ten minutes, and it was a marvel to me how he managed to do it. Then the great moment came, and Anderson closed the firing circuit. The bomb started to cook, building up pressure inside as the sodium volatilized. After thirty seconds, there was a sudden puff of smoke from the long, slender nozzle pointing up at the sky. And then we had to wait for another ten minutes while the invisible cloud rose to the stars. After all this build-up, I told myself, the result had better be good.

The seconds and minutes ebbed away. Then a sudden yellow glow began to spread across the sky, like a vast and unwavering aurora that became brighter even as we watched. It was as if an artist was sprawling strokes across the stars with a flame-filled brush. And as I stared at those strokes, I suddenly realized that someone had brought off the greatest advertising coup in history. For the strokes formed letters, and the letters formed two words—the name of a certain soft drink too well known to need any further publicity from me.

How had it been done? The first answer was obvious. Someone had placed a suitably cut stencil in the nozzle of the sodium bomb, so that the stream of escaping vapor had shaped itself to the words. Since there was nothing to distort it, the pattern had kept its shape during its invisible ascent to the stars. I had seen skywriting on Earth, but this was something on a far larger scale. Whatever I thought of them, I couldn't help admiring the ingenuity of the men who had perpetrated the scheme. The O's and A's had given them a bit of trouble, but the C's and L's were perfect.

After the initial shock, I am glad to say that the scientific program proceeded as planned. I wish I could remember how Dave Bolton rose to the occasion in his commentary; it must have been a strain even for his quick wits. By this time, of course, half the Earth could see what he was describing. The next morning, every newspaper on the planet carried that famous photo of the crescent moon with the luminous slogan painted across its darkened sector.

The letters were visible, before they finally dispersed into space, for over an hour. By that time the words were almost a thousand miles long, and were beginning to get blurred. But they were still readable until they at last faded from sight in the ultimate vacuum between the planets.

Then the real fireworks began. Commander Vandenburg was absolutely furious, and promptly started to grill all his men. However, it was soon clear that the saboteur—if you could call him that—had been back on Earth. The bomb had been prepared there and shipped ready for immediate use. It did not take long to find, and fire, the engineer who had carried out the substitution. He couldn't have cared less, since his financial needs had been taken care of for a good many years to come.

As for the experiment itself, it was completely successful from the scientific point of view; all the recording instruments worked perfectly as they analyzed the light from the unexpectedly shaped cloud. But we never let the Americans live it down, and I am afraid poor Captain Vandenburg was the one who suffered most. Before he came to the moon he was a confirmed teetotaler, and much of his refreshment came from a certain wasp-waisted bottle. But now, as a matter of principle, he can only drink beer—and he hates the stuff.

I HAVE ALREADY described the—shall we say—jockeying for position before take-off on the first flight to the moon. As it turned out, the American, Russian, and British ships landed just about simultaneously. No one has ever explained, however, why the British ship came back nearly two weeks after the others.

Oh, I know the official story; I ought to, for I helped to concoct it. It is true as far it goes, but it scarcely goes far enough.

On all counts, the joint expedition had been a triumphant success. There had been only one casualty, and in the manner of his death Vladimir Surov had made himself immortal. We had gathered knowledge that would keep the scientists of Earth busy for generations, and that would revolutionize almost all our ideas concerning the nature of the universe around us. Yes, our five months on the moon had been well spent, and we could go home to such welcomes as few heroes had ever had before.

However, there was still a good deal of tidying up to be done. The instruments that had been scattered all over the lunar landscape were still busily recording, and much of the information they gathered could not be automatically radioed back to Earth. There was no point in all three of the expeditions staying on the moon to the last minute; the personnel of one would be sufficient to finish the job. But who would volunteer to be caretaker while the others went back to gain the glory? It was a difficult problem, but one that would have to be solved very soon.

As far as supplies were concerned, we had little to worry about. The automatic freight rockets could keep us provided with air, food, and water for as long as we wished to stay on the moon. We were all in good health, though a little tired. None of the anticipated psychological troubles had cropped up, perhaps because we had all been so busy on tasks of absorbing interest that we had had no time to worry about going crazy. But, of course, we all looked forward to getting back to Earth and seeing our families again.

The first change of plan was forced upon us by the *Ziolkovski* being put out of commission when the ground beneath one of her landing legs suddenly gave way. The ship managed to stay upright, but the hull was badly twisted and the pressure cabin sprang dozens of leaks. There was much debate about on-the-spot repairs, but it was decided that it would be far too risky for her to take off in this condition. The Russians had no alternative but to thumb lifts back in the *Goddard* and the *Endeavour;* by using the *Ziolkovski's* unwanted fuel, our ships would be able to manage the extra load. However, the return flight would be extremely cramped and uncomfortable for all concerned because everyone would have to eat and sleep in shifts.

Either the American or the British ship, therefore, would be the first back to Earth. During those final weeks, as the work of the expedition was brought to its close, relations between Commander Vandenburg and myself were somewhat strained. I even wondered if we ought to settle the matter by tossing for it. . . .

Another problem was also engaging my attention—that of crew discipline. Perhaps this is too strong a phrase; I would not like it to be thought that a mutiny ever seemed probable. But all my men were now a little abstracted and liable to be found, if off duty, scribbling furiously in corners. I knew exactly what was going on, for I was involved in it myself. There wasn't a human being on the moon who had not sold exclusive rights to some newspaper or magazine, and we were all haunted by approaching deadlines. The radio-teletype to Earth was in continuous operation, sending tens of thousands of words being dictated over the speech circuits.

It was Professor Williams, our very practical-minded astronomer, who came to me one day with the answer to my main problem.

"Skipper," he said, balancing himself precariously on the all-too-collapsible table I used as my working desk inside the igloo, "there's no technical reason, is there, why we should get back to Earth first?"

"No," I said, "merely a matter of fame, fortune, and seeing our families again. But I admit those aren't technical reasons. We could stay here another year if Earth kept sending supplies. If you want to suggest that, however, I shall take great pleasure in strangling you."

"It's not as bad as that. Once the main body has gone back, whichever party is left can follow in two or three weeks at the latest. They'll get a lot of credit, in fact, for self-sacrifice, modesty, and similar virtues."

"Which will be very poor compensation for being second home."

"Right—we need something else to make it worth-while. Some more material reward."

"Agreed. What do you suggest?"

Williams pointed to the calendar hanging on the wall in front of me, between the two pin-ups we had stolen from the *Goddard*. The length of our stay was indicated by the days that had been crossed off in red ink; a big question mark in two weeks' time showed when the first ship would be heading back to Earth.

"There's your answer," he said. "If we go back then, do you realize what will happen? I'll tell you."

He did, and I kicked myself for not having thought of it first.

The next day, I explained my decision to Vandenburg and Krasnin.

"We'll stay behind and do the mopping up," I said. "It's a matter of common sense. The *Goddard*'s a much bigger ship than ours and can carry an extra four people, while we can manage only two more, and even then it will be a squeeze. If you go first, Van, it will save a lot of people from eating their hearts out here for longer than necessary."

"That's very big of you," replied Vandenburg. "I won't hide the fact that we'll be happy to get home. And it's logical, I admit, now that the *Ziolkovski*'s out of action. Still, it means quite a sacrifice on your part, and I don't really like to take advantage of it."

I gave an expansive wave.

"Think nothing of it," I answered. "As long as you boys don't grab all the credit, we'll take our turn. After all, we'll have the show here to ourselves when you've gone back to Earth."

Krasnin was looking at me with a rather calculating expression, and I found it singularly difficult to return his gaze.

"I hate to sound cynical," he said, "but I've learned to be a little suspicious when people start doing big favors without very good reasons. And frankly, I don't think the reason you've given is good enough. You wouldn't have anything else up your sleeve, would you?"

"Oh, very well," I sighed. "I'd hoped to get a *little* credit, but I see it's no use trying to convince anyone of the purity of my motives. I've got a reason, and you might as well know it. But please don't spread it around; I'd hate the folks back on Earth to be disillusioned. They still think of us as noble and heroic seekers after knowledge; let's keep it that way, for all our sakes."

Then I pulled out the calendar, and explained to Vandenburg and Krasnin what Williams had already explained to me. They listened with skepticism, then with growing sympathy.

"I had no idea it was *that* bad," said Vandenburg at last.

"Americans never have," I said sadly. "Anyway, that's the way it's been for half a century, and it doesn't seem to get any better. So you agree with my suggestion?"

"Of course. It suits us fine, anyhow. Until the next expedition's ready, the moon's all yours."

I remembered that phrase, two weeks later, as I watched the *Goddard* blast up into the sky toward the distant, beckoning Earth. It was lonely, then, when the Americans and all but two of the Russians had gone. We envied them the reception they got, and watched jealously on the TV screens their triumphant processions through Moscow and New York. Then we went back to work, and bided our time. Whenever we felt depressed, we would do little sums on bits of paper and would be instantly restored to cheerfulness.

The red crosses marched across the calendar as the short terrestrial days went by—days that seemed to have very little connection with the slow cycle of lunar time. At last we were ready; all the instrument readings were taken, all the specimens and samples safely packed away aboard the ship. The motors roared into life, giving us for a moment the weight we would feel again when we were back in Earth's gravity. Below us the rugged lunar landscape, which we had grown to know so well, fell swiftly away; within seconds we could see no sign at all of the buildings and instruments we had so laboriously erected and which future explorers would one day use.

The homeward voyage had begun. We returned to Earth in uneventful discomfort, joined the already half-dismantled *Goddard* beside Space Station Three, and were quickly ferried down to the world we had left seven months before.

*Seven months:* that, as Williams had pointed out, was the all-important figure. We had been on the moon for more than half a financial year—and for all of us, it had been the most profitable year of our lives.

Sooner or later, I suppose, this interplanetary loophole will be plugged; the Department of Inland Revenue is still fighting a gallant rear-guard action, but we seem neatly covered under Section 57, paragraph 8 of the Capital Gains Act of 1972. We wrote our books and articles on the moon—and until there's a lunar government to impose income tax, we're hanging on to every penny.

And if the ruling finally goes against us—well, there's always Mars. . . .

THE CONCUSSION of the last atom bomb still seemed to linger as the lights came on again. For a long time, no one moved. Then the assistant producer said innocently: "Well, R.B., what do you think of it?"

R.B. heaved himself out of his seat while his acolytes waited to see which way the cat would jump. It was then that they noticed that R.B.'s cigar had gone out. Why, that hadn't happened even at the preview of "G.W.T.W."!

"Boys," he said ecstatically, "we've got something here! How much did you say it cost, Mike?"

"Six and a half million, R.B."

"It was cheap at the price. Let me tell you, I'll eat every foot of it if the gross doesn't beat 'Quo Vadis.' " He wheeled, as swiftly as could be expected for one of his bulk, upon a small man still crouched in his seat at the back of the projection room. "Snap out of it, Joe! The Earth's saved! You've seen all these space films. How does this line up with the earlier ones?"

Joe came to with an obvious effort.

"There's no comparison," he said. "It's got all the suspense of 'The Thing,' without that awful letdown at the end when you saw the monster was human. The only picture that comes within miles of it is 'War of the Worlds.' Some of the effects in that were nearly as good as ours, but of course George Pal didn't have 3 D. And that sure makes a difference! When the Golden Gate Bridge went down, I thought that pier was going to hit me!"

"The bit I liked best," put in Tony Auerbach from Publicity, "was when the Empire State Building split right up the middle. You don't suppose the owners might sue us, though?"

"Of course not. No one expects *any* building to stand up to—what did the script call them?—city busters. And, after all, we wiped out the rest of New York as well. Ugh—that scene in the Holland Tunnel when the roof gave way! Next time, I'll take the ferry!"

"Yes, that was very well done—almost *too* well done. But what really got me was those creatures from space. The animation was perfect—how did you do it, Mike?"

"Trade secret," said the proud producer. "Still, I'll let you in on it. A lot of that stuff is genuine."

"What!"

"Oh, don't get me wrong! We haven't been on location to Sirius B. But they've developed a microcamera over at Cal Tech, and we used that to film spiders in action. We cut in the best shots, and I think you'd have a job telling which was micro and which was the full-sized studio stuff. Now you understand why I wanted the Aliens to be insects, and not octopuses, like the script said first."

"There's a good publicity angle here," said Tony. "One thing worries me, though. That scene where the monsters kidnap Gloria. Do you suppose the censor . . . I mean the way we've done it, it almost looks . . ."

"Aw, quit worrying! *That's* what people are supposed to think! Anyway, we make it clear in the next reel that they really want her for dissection, so that's all right."

"It'll be a riot!" gloated R.B., a faraway gleam in his eye as if he was already hearing the avalanche of dollars pouring into the box office. "Look—we'll put another million into publicity! I can just see the posters—get all this down, Tony. WATCH THE SKY! THE SIRIANS ARE COMING! And we'll make thousands of clockwork models—can't you imagine them scuttling around on their hairy legs! People love to be scared, and we'll scare them. By the time we've finished, no one will be able to look at the sky without getting the creeps! I leave it to you, boys—this picture is going to make *history*!"

He was right. "Monsters from Space" hit the public two months later. Within a week of the simultaneous London and New York *premières,* there could have been no one in the western world who had not seen the posters screaming EARTH BEWARE! or had not shuddered at the photographs of the hairy horrors stalking along deserted Fifth Avenue on their thin, many-jointed legs. Blimps cleverly disguised as spaceships cruised across the skies, to the vast confusion of pilots who encountered them, and clockwork models of the Alien invaders were everywhere, scaring old ladies out of their wits.

The publicity campaign was brilliant, and the picture would undoubtedly have run for months had it not been for a coincidence as disastrous as it was unforeseeable. While the number of people fainting at each performance was still news, the skies of Earth filled suddenly with long, lean shadows sliding swiftly through the clouds. . . .

●

Prince Zervashni was good-natured but inclined to be impetuous—a well-known failing of his race. There was no reason to suppose that his present mission, that of making peaceful contact with the planet Earth, would present any particular problems. The correct technique of approach had been thoroughly worked out over many thousands of years, as the Third Galactic Empire slowly expanded its frontiers, absorbing planet after planet, sun upon sun. There was seldom any trouble: really intelligent races can always co-operate, once they have got over the initial shock of learning that they are not alone in the universe.

It was true that humanity had emerged from its primitive, warlike stage only within the last generation. This, however, did not worry Prince Zervashni's chief adviser, Sigisnin II, Professor of Astropolitics.

"It's a perfectly typical Class E culture," said the professor. "Technically advanced, morally rather backward. However, they are already used to the conception of space flight, and will soon take us for granted. The normal precautions will be sufficient until we have won their confidence."

"Very well," said the prince. "Tell the envoys to leave at once."

It was unfortunate that the "normal precautions" did not allow for Tony Auerbach's publicity campaign, which had now reached new heights of interplanetary xenophobia. The ambassadors landed in New York's Central Park on the very day that a prominent astronomer, unusually hard up and therefore amenable to influence, announced in a widely reported interview that any visitors from space probably would be unfriendly.

The luckless ambassadors, heading for the United Nations Building, had got as far south as 60th Street when they met the mob. The encounter was very one-sided, and the scientists at the Museum of Natural History were most annoyed that there was so little left for them to examine.

Prince Zervashni tried once more, on the other side of the planet, but the news had got there first. This time the ambassadors were armed, and gave a good account of themselves before they were overwhelmed by sheer numbers. Even so, it was not until the rocket bombs started climbing up toward his fleet that the prince finally lost his temper and decided to take drastic action.

It was all over in twenty minutes, and was really quite painless. Then the prince turned to his adviser and said, with considerable understatement: "That appears to be that. And now—can you tell me exactly what went wrong?"

Sigisnin II knitted his dozen flexible fingers together in acute anguish. It was not only the spectacle of the neatly disinfected Earth that distressed him, though to a scientist the destruction of such a beautiful specimen is always a major tragedy. At least equally upsetting was the demolition of his theories and, with them, his reputation.

"I just don't understand it!" he lamented. "Of course, races at this level of culture are often suspicious and nervous when contact is first made. But they'd never had visitors before, so there was no reason for them to be hostile."

"Hostile! They were demons! I think they were all insane." The prince turned to his captain, a tripedal creature who looked rather like a ball of wool balanced on three knitting needles.

"Is the fleet reassembled?"

"Yes, Sire."

"Then we will return to Base at optimum speed. This planet depresses me."

On the dead and silent Earth, the posters still screamed their warnings from a thousand hoardings. The malevolent insectile shapes shown pouring from the skies bore no resemblance at all to Prince Zervashni, who apart from his four eyes might have been mistaken for a panda with purple fur —and who, moreover, had come from Rigel, not Sirius.

But, of course, it was now much too late to point this out.

## ALL THE TIME IN THE WORLD

WHEN THE QUIET KNOCK came on the door, Robert Ashton surveyed the room in one swift, automatic movement. Its dull respectability satisfied him and should reassure any visitor. Not that he had any reason to expect the police, but there was no point in taking chances.

"Come in," he said, pausing only to grab Plato's *Dialogues* from the shelf beside him. Perhaps this gesture was a little too ostentatious, but it always impressed his clients.

The door opened slowly. At first, Ashton continued his intent reading, not bothering to glance up. There was the slightest acceleration of his heart, a mild and even exhilarating constriction of the chest. Of course, it couldn't possibly be a flatfoot: someone would have tipped him off. Still, any unheralded visitor was unusual and thus potentially dangerous.

Ashton laid down the book, glanced toward the door and remarked in a noncommittal voice: "What can I do for you?" He did not get up; such courtesies belonged to a past he had buried long ago. Besides, it was a woman. In the circles he now frequented, women were accustomed to receive jewels and clothes and money—but never respect.

Yet there was something about this visitor that drew him slowly to his feet. It was not merely that she was beautiful, but she had a poised and effortless authority that moved her into a different world from the flamboyant doxies he met in the normal course of business. There was a brain and a purpose behind those calm, appraising eyes—a brain, Ashton suspected, the equal of his own.

He did not know how grossly he had underestimated her.

"Mr. Ashton," she began, "let us not waste time. I know who you are and I have work for you. Here are my credentials."

She opened a large, stylish handbag and extracted a thick bundle of notes.

"You may regard this," she said, "as a sample."

Ashton caught the bundle as she tossed it carelessly toward him. It was the largest sum of money he had ever held in his life—at least a hundred fivers, all new and serially numbered. He felt them between his fingers. If they were not genuine, they were so good that the difference was of no practical importance.

He ran his thumb to and fro along the edge of the wad as if feeling a pack for a marked card, and said thoughtfully, "I'd like to know where you got these. If they aren't forgeries, they must be hot and will take some passing."

"They are genuine. A very short time ago they were in the Bank of England. But if they are of no use to you throw them in the fire. I merely let you have them to show that I mean business."

"Go on." He gestured to the only seat and balanced himself on the edge of the table.

She drew a sheaf of papers from the capacious handbag and handed it across to him.

"I am prepared to pay you any sum you wish if you will secure these items and bring them to me, at a time and place to be arranged. What is more, I will guarantee that you can make the thefts with no personal danger."

Ashton looked at the list, and sighed. The woman was

mad. Still, she had better be humored. There might be more money where this came from.

"I notice," he said mildly, "that all these items are in the British Museum, and that most of them are, quite literally, priceless. By that I mean that you could neither buy nor sell them."

"I do not wish to sell them. I am a collector."

"So it seems. What are you prepared to pay for these acquisitions?"

"Name a figure."

There was a short silence. Ashton weighed the possibilities. He took a certain professional pride in his work, but there were some things that no amount of money could accomplish. Still, it would be amusing to see how high the bidding would go.

He looked at the list again.

"I think a round million would be a very reasonable figure for this lot," he said ironically.

"I fear you are not taking me very seriously. With your contacts, you should be able to dispose of these."

There was a flash of light and something sparkled through the air. Ashton caught the necklace before it hit the ground, and despite himself was unable to suppress a gasp of amazement. A fortune glittered through his fingers. The central diamond was the largest he had ever seen—it must be one of the world's most famous jewels.

His visitor seemed completely indifferent as he slipped the necklace into his pocket. Ashton was badly shaken; he knew she was not acting. To her, that fabulous gem was of no more value than a lump of sugar. This was madness on an unimaginable scale.

"Assuming that you can deliver the money," he said, "how do you imagine that it's physically possible to do what you ask? One might steal a single item from this list, but within a few hours the Museum would be solid with police."

With a fortune already in his pocket, he could afford to be frank. Besides, he was curious to learn more about his fantastic visitor.

She smiled, rather sadly, as if humoring a backward child. "If I show you the way," she said softly, "will you do it?"

"Yes—for a million."

"Have you noticed anything strange since I came in? Is it not—very quiet?"

Ashton listened. My God, she was right! This room was never completely silent, even at night. There had been a wind blowing over the roof tops; where had it gone now? The distant rumble of traffic had ceased; five minutes ago he had been cursing the engines shunting in the marshaling yard at the end of the road. What had happened to them?

"Go to the window."

He obeyed the order and drew aside the grimy lace curtains with fingers that shook slightly despite all attempt at control. Then he relaxed. The street was quite empty, as it often was at this time in the midmorning. There was no traffic, and hence no reason for sound. Then he glanced down the row of dingy houses toward the shunting yard.

His visitor smiled as he stiffened with the shock.

"Tell me what you see, Mr. Ashton."

He turned slowly, face pale and throat muscles working. "What are you?" he gasped. "A witch?"

"Don't be foolish. There is a simple explanation. It is not the world that has changed—but you."

Ashton stared again at that unbelievable shunting engine, the plume of steam frozen motionless above it as if made from cotton wool. He realized now that the clouds were equally immobile; they should have been scudding across the sky. All around him was the unnatural stillness of the high-speed photograph, the vivid unreality of a scene glimpsed in a flash of lightning.

"You are intelligent enough to realize what is happening, even if you cannot understand how it is done. Your time scale has been altered: a minute in the outer world would be a year in this room."

Again she opened the handbag, and this time brought forth what appeared to be a bracelet of some silvery metal, with a series of dials and switches molded into it.

"You can call this a personal generator," she said. "With it strapped about your arm, you are invincible. You can come and go without hindrance—you can steal everything on that list and bring it to me before one of the guards in the Museum has blinked an eyelid. When you have finished, you can be miles away before you switch off the field and step back into the normal world.

"Now listen carefully, and do exactly what I say. The field has a radius of about seven feet, so you must keep at least that distance from any other person. Secondly, you must not switch it off again until you have completed your task and I have given you your payment. *This is most important.* Now, the plan I have worked out is this. . . ."

No criminal in the history of the world had ever possessed such power. It was intoxicating—yet Ashton wondered if he would ever get used to it. He had ceased to worry about explanations, at least until the job was done and he had collected his reward. Then, perhaps, he would get away from England and enjoy a well-earned retirement.

His visitor had left a few minutes ahead of him, but when he stepped out into the street the scene was completely unchanged. Though he had prepared for it, the sensation was still unnerving. Ashton felt an impulse to hurry, as if this condition couldn't possibly last and he had to get the job done before the gadget ran out of juice. But that, he had been assured, was impossible.

In the High Street he slowed down to look at the frozen traffic, the paralyzed pedestrians. He was careful, as he had been warned, not to approach so close to anyone that they came within his field. How ridiculous people looked when one saw them like this, robbed of such grace as movement could give, their mouths half open in foolish grimaces!

Having to seek assistance went against the grain, but some parts of the job were too big for him to handle by himself. Besides, he could pay liberally and never notice it. The main difficulty, Ashton realized, would be to find someone who was intelligent enough not to be scared—or so stupid that he would take everything for granted. He decided to try the first possibility.

Tony Marchetti's place was down a side street so close to the police station that one felt it was really carrying camouflage too far. As he walked past the entrance, Ashton caught a glimpse of the duty sergeant at his desk and resisted a temptation to go inside to combine a little pleasure with business. But that sort of thing could wait until later.

The door of Tony's opened in his face as he approached. It was such a natural occurrence in a world where nothing was normal that it was a moment before Ashton realized its implications. Had his generator failed? He glanced hastily down the street and was reassured by the frozen tableau behind him.

"Well, if it isn't Bob Ashton!" said a familiar voice. "Fancy meeting you as early in the morning as this. That's an odd bracelet you're wearing. I thought I had the only one."

"Hello, Aram," replied Ashton. "It looks as if there's a lot going on that neither of us knows about. Have you signed up Tony, or is he still free?"

"Sorry. We've a little job which will keep him busy for a while."

"Don't tell me. It's at the National Gallery or the Tate."

Aram Albenkian fingered his neat goatee. "Who told you that?" he asked.

"No one. But, after all, you *are* the crookedest art dealer in the trade, and I'm beginning to guess what's going on. Did a tall, very good-looking brunette give you that bracelet and a shopping list?"

"I don't see why I should tell you, but the answer's no. It was a man."

Ashton felt a momentary surprise. Then he shrugged his shoulders. "I might have guessed that there would be more than one of them. I'd like to know who's behind it."

"Have you any theories?" said Albenkian guardedly.

Ashton decided that it would be worth risking some loss of information to test the other's reactions. "It's obvious they're not interested in money—they have all they want and can get more with this gadget. The woman who saw me said she was a collector. I took it as a joke, but I see now that she meant it seriously."

"Why do we come into the picture? What's to stop them doing the whole job themselves?" Albenkian asked.

"Maybe they're frightened. Or perhaps they want our—er—specialized knowledge. Some of the items on my list are rather well cased in. My theory is that they're agents for a mad millionaire."

It didn't hold water, and Ashton knew it. But he wanted to see which leaks Albenkian would try to plug.

"My dear Ashton," said the other impatiently, holding up his wrist. "How do you explain this little thing? I know nothing about science, but even I can tell that it's beyond the wildest dreams of our technologies. There's only one conclusion to be drawn from that."

"Go on."

"These people are from—somewhere else. Our world is being systematically looted of its treasures. You know all this stuff you read about rockets and spaceships? Well, someone else has done it first."

Ashton didn't laugh. The theory was no more fantastic than the facts.

"Whoever they are," he said, "they seem to know their way around pretty well. I wonder how many teams they've got? Perhaps the Louvre and the Prado are being reconnoitered at this very minute. The world is going to have a shock before the day's out."

They parted amicably enough, neither confiding any details of real importance about his business. For a fleeting moment Ashton thought of trying to buy over Tony, but there was no point in antagonizing Albenkian. Steve Regan would have to do. That meant walking about a mile, since of course any form of transport was impossible. He would die of old age before a bus completed the journey. Ashton was not clear what would happen if he attempted to drive a car when the field was operating, and he had been warned not to try any experiments.

It astonished Ashton that even such a nearly certified moron as Steve could take the accelerator so calmly; there was something to be said, after all, for the comic strips which were probably his only reading. After a few words of grossly simplified explanation, Steve buckled on the spare wristlet which, rather to Ashton's surprise, his visitor had handed over without comment. Then they set out on their long walk to the Museum.

Ashton, or his client, had thought of everything. They stopped once at a park bench to rest and enjoy some sandwiches and regain their breath. When at last they reached the Museum, neither felt any the worse for the unaccustomed exercise.

They walked together through the gates of the Museum —unable, despite logic, to avoid speaking in whispers—and up the wide stone steps into the entrance hall. Ashton knew his way perfectly. With whimsical humor he displayed his Reading Room ticket as they walked, at a respectful distance, past the statuesque attendants. It occurred to him that the occupants of the great chamber, for the most part, looked just the same as they normally did, even without the benefit of the accelerator.

It was a straightforward but tedious job collecting the books that had been listed. They had been chosen, it seemed, for their beauty as works of art as much as for their literary content. The selection had been done by someone who knew his job. Had *they* done it themselves, Ashton wondered, or had they bribed other experts as they were bribing him? He wondered if he would ever glimpse the full ramifications of their plot.

There was a considerable amount of panel-smashing to be done, but Ashton was careful not to damage any books, even the unwanted ones. Whenever he had collected enough volumes to make a comfortable load, Steve carried them out into the courtyard and dumped them on the paving stones until a small pyramid had accumulated.

It would not matter if they were left for short periods

outside the field of the accelerator. No one would notice their momentary flicker of existence in the normal world.

They were in the library for two hours of their time, and paused for another snack before passing to the next job. On the way Ashton stopped for a little private business. There was a tinkle of glass as the tiny case, standing in solitary splendor, yielded up its treasure: then the manuscript of *Alice* was safely tucked into Ashton's pocket.

Among the antiquities, he was not quite so much at home. There were a few examples to be taken from every gallery, and sometimes it was hard to see the reasons for the choice. It was as if—and again he remembered Albenkian's words—these works of art had been selected by someone with totally alien standards. This time, with a few exceptions, *they* had obviously not been guided by the experts.

For the second time in history the case of the Portland Vase was shattered. In five seconds, thought Ashton, the alarms would be going all over the Museum and the whole building would be in an uproar. And in five seconds he could be miles away. It was an intoxicating thought, and as he worked swiftly to complete his contract he began to regret the price he had asked. Even now, it was not too late.

He felt the quiet satisfaction of the good workman as he watched Steve carry the great silver tray of the Mildenhall Treasure out into the courtyard and place it beside the now impressive pile. "That's the lot," he said. "I'll settle up at my place this evening. Now let's get this gadget off you."

They walked out into High Holborn and chose a secluded side street that had no pedestrians near it. Ashton unfastened the peculiar buckle and stepped back from his cohort, watching him freeze into immobility as he did so. Steve was vulnerable again, moving once more with all other men in the stream of time. But before the alarm had gone out he would have lost himself in the London crowds.

When he re-entered the Museum yard, the treasure had already gone. Standing where it had been was his visitor of —how long ago? She was still poised and graceful, but, Ashton thought, looking a little tired. He approached until their fields merged and they were no longer separated by an impassable gulf of silence. "I hope you're satisfied," he said. "How did you move the stuff so quickly?"

She touched the bracelet around her own wrist and gave a wan smile. "We have many other powers besides this."

"Then why did you need my help?"

"There were technical reasons. It was necessary to remove the objects we required from the presence of other matter.

In this way, we could gather only what we needed and not waste our limited—what shall I call them?—transporting facilities. Now may I have the bracelet back?"

Ashton slowly handed over the one he was carrying, but made no effort to unfasten his own. There might be danger in what he was doing, but he intended to retreat at the first sign of it.

"I'm prepared to reduce my fee," he said. "In fact I'll waive all payment—in exchange for this." He touched his wrist, where the intricate metal band gleamed in the sunlight.

She was watching him with an expression as fathomless as the Gioconda smile. (Had *that*, Ashton wondered, gone to join the treasure he had gathered? How much had they taken from the Louvre?)

"I would not call that reducing your fee. All the money in the world could not purchase one of those bracelets."

"Or the things I have given you."

"You are greedy, Mr. Ashton. You know that with an accelerator the entire world would be yours."

"What of that? Do you have any further interest in our planet, now you have taken what you need?"

There was a pause. Then, unexpectedly, she smiled. "So you have guessed I do not belong to your world."

"Yes. And I know that you have other agents besides myself. Do you come from Mars, or won't you tell me?"

"I am quite willing to tell you. But you may not thank me if I do."

Ashton looked at her warily. What did she mean by that? Unconscious of his action, he put his wrist behind his back, protecting the bracelet.

"No, I am not from Mars, or any planet of which you have ever heard. You would not understand *what* I am. Yet I will tell you this. I am from the Future."

"The Future! That's ridiculous!"

"Indeed? I should be interested to know why."

"If that sort of thing were possible, our past history would be full of time travelers. Besides, it would involve a *reductio ad absurdum*. Going into the past could change the present and produce all sorts of paradoxes."

"Those are good points, though not perhaps as original as you suppose. But they only refute the possibility of time travel in general, not in the very special case which concerns us now."

"What is peculiar about it?" he asked.

"On very rare occasions, and by the release of an enormous amount of energy, it is possible to produce a—*singularity*—

in time. During the fraction of a second when that singularity occurs, the past becomes accessible to the future, though only in a restricted way. We can send our minds back to you, but not our bodies."

"You mean," said Ashton, "that you are *borrowing* the body I see?"

"Oh, I have paid for it, as I am paying you. The owner has agreed to the terms. We are very conscientious in these matters."

Ashton was thinking swiftly. If this story was true, it gave him a definite advantage.

"You mean," he continued, "that you have no direct control over matter, and must work through human agents?"

"Yes. Even those bracelets were made here, under our mental control."

She was explaining too much too readily, revealing all her weaknesses. A warning signal was flashing in the back of Ashton's mind, but he had committed himself too deeply to retreat.

"Then it seems to me," he said slowly, "that you cannot force me to hand this bracelet back."

"That is perfectly true."

"That's all I want to know."

She was smiling at him now, and there was something in that smile that chilled him to the marrow.

"We are not vindictive or unkind, Mr. Ashton," she said quietly. "What I am going to do now appeals to my sense of justice. You have asked for that bracelet; you can keep it. Now I shall tell you just how useful it will be."

For a moment Ashton had a wild impulse to hand back the accelerator. She must have guessed his thoughts.

"No, it's too late. I insist that you keep it. And I can reassure you on one point. It won't wear out. It will last you"—again that enigmatic smile—"the rest of your life.

"Do you mind if we go for a walk, Mr. Ashton? I have done my work here, and would like to have a last glimpse of your world before I leave it forever."

She turned toward the iron gates, and did not wait for a reply. Consumed by curiosity, Ashton followed.

They walked in silence until they were standing among the frozen traffic of Tottenham Court Road. For a while she stood staring at the busy yet motionless crowds; then she sighed.

"I cannot help feeling sorry for them, and for you. I wonder what you would have made of yourselves."

"What do you mean by that?"

"Just now, Mr. Ashton, you implied that the future cannot reach back into the past, because that would alter history. A shrewd remark, but, I am afraid, irrelevant. You see, *your* world has no more history to alter."

She pointed across the road, and Ashton turned swiftly on his heels. There was nothing there except a newsboy crouching over his pile of papers. A placard formed an impossible curve in the breeze that was blowing through this motionless world. Ashton read the crudely lettered words with difficulty:

## SUPER-BOMB TEST TODAY

The voice in his ears seemed to come from a very long way off.

"I told you that time travel, even in this restricted form, requires an enormous release of energy—far more than a single bomb can liberate, Mr. Ashton. But that bomb is only a trigger—"

She pointed to the solid ground beneath their feet. "Do you know anything about your own planet? Probably not; your race has learned so little. But even your scientists have discovered that, two thousand miles down, the Earth has a dense, liquid core. That core is made of compressed matter, and it can exist in either of two stable states. Given a certain stimulus, it can change from one of those states to another, just as a seesaw can tip over at the touch of a finger. But that change, Mr. Ashton, will liberate as much energy as all the earthquakes since the beginning of your world. The oceans and continents will fly into space; the sun will have a second asteroid belt.

"That cataclysm will send its echoes down the ages, and will open up to us a fraction of a second in your time. During that instant, we are trying to save what we can of your world's treasures. It is all that we can do; even if your motives were purely selfish and completely dishonest, you have done your race a service you never intended.

"And now I must return to our ship, where it waits by the ruins of Earth almost a hundred thousand years from now. You can keep the bracelet."

The withdrawal was instantaneous. The woman suddenly froze and became one with the other statues in the silent street. He was alone.

Alone! Ashton held the gleaming bracelet before his eyes, hypnotized by its intricate workmanship and by the powers it concealed. He had made a bargain, and he must keep it. He could live out the full span of his life—at the cost of an isolation no other man had ever known. If he switched off the field, the last seconds of history would tick inexorably away.

*Seconds?* Indeed, there was less time than that. For he knew that the bomb must already have exploded.

He sat down on the edge of the pavement and began to think. There was no need to panic; he must take things calmly, without hysteria. After all, he had plenty of time.

All the time in the world.

## COSMIC CASANOVA

THIS TIME I was five weeks out from Base Planet before the symptoms became acute. On the last trip it had taken only a month; I was not certain whether the difference was due to advancing age or to something the dietitians had put into my food capsules. Or it could merely have been that I was busier; the arm of the galaxy I was scouting was heavily populated, with stars only a couple of light-years apart, so I had little time to brood over the girls I'd left behind me. As soon as one star had been classified, and the automatic search for planets had been completed, it was time to head for the next sun. And when, as happened in about one case out of ten, planets *did* turn up, I'd be furiously busy for several days seeing that Max, the ship's electronic computer, got all the information down on his tapes.

Now, however, I was through this densely packed region of space, and it sometimes took as much as three days to get from sun to sun. That was time enough for Sex to come tiptoeing aboard the ship, and for the memories of my last leave to make the months ahead look very empty indeed.

Perhaps I had overdone it, back on Diadne V, while my ship was being reprovisioned and I was supposed to be resting between missions. But a survey scout spends eighty per cent of his time alone in space, and human nature being what it is, he must be expected to make up for lost time. I had not merely done that; I'd built up considerable credit for the future—though not, it seemed, enough to last me through this trip.

First, I recalled wistfully, there had been Helene. She was

blonde, cuddly, and compliant, though rather unimaginative. We had a fine time together until her husband came back from *his* mission; he was extremely decent about it but pointed out, reasonably enough, that Helene would now have very little time for other engagements. Fortunately, I had already made contact with Iris, so the hiatus was negligible.

Now Iris was really something. Even now, it makes me squirm to think of her. When that affair broke up—for the simple reason that a man has to get a little sleep sometime— I swore off women for a whole week. Then I came across a touching poem by an old Earth writer named John Donne —he's worth looking up, if you can read Primitive English— which reminded me that time lost could never be regained.

How true, I thought, so I put on my spaceman's uniform and wandered down to the beach of Diadne V's only sea. There was need to walk no more than a few hundred meters before I'd spotted a dozen possibilities, brushed off several volunteers, and signed up Natalie.

That worked out pretty well at first, until Natalie started objecting to Ruth (or was it Kay?). I can't *stand* girls who think they own a man, so I blasted off after a rather difficult scene that was quite expensive in crockery. This left me at loose ends for a couple of days; then Cynthia came to the rescue and—but by now you'll have gotten the general idea, so I won't bore you with details.

These, then, were the fond memories I started to work back through while one star dwindled behind me and the next flared up ahead. On this trip I'd deliberately left my pin-ups behind, having decided that they only made matters worse. This was a mistake; being quite a good artist in a rather specialized way, I started to draw my own, and it wasn't long before I had a collection it would be hard to match on any respectable planet.

I would hate you to think that this preoccupation affected my efficiency as a unit of the Galactic Survey. It was only on the long, dull runs between the stars, when I had no one to talk to but the computer, that I found my glands getting the better of me. Max, my electronic colleague, was good enough company in the ordinary course of events, but there are some things that a machine can't be expected to understand. I often hurt his feelings when I was in one of my irritable moods and lost my temper for no apparent reason. "What's the matter, Joe?" Max would say plaintively. "Surely you're not mad at me because I beat you at chess again? Remember, I warned you I would."

"Oh, go to hell!" I'd snarl back—and then I'd have an anxious five minutes while I straightened things out with the rather literal-minded Navigation Robot.

Two months out from Base, with thirty suns and four solar systems logged, something happened that wiped all my personal problems from my mind. The long-range monitor began to beep; a faint signal was coming from somewhere in the section of space ahead of me. I got the most accurate bearing that I could; the transmission was unmodulated, very narrow band—clearly a beacon of some kind. Yet no ship of ours, to the best of my knowledge, had ever entered this remote neck of the universe; I was supposed to be scouting completely unexplored territory.

This, I told myself, is IT—my big moment, the payoff for all the lonely years I'd spent in space. At some unknown distance ahead of me was another civilization—a race sufficiently advanced to possess hyper-radio.

I knew exactly what I had to do. As soon as Max had confirmed my readings and made his analysis, I launched a message carrier back to Base. If anything happened to me, the Survey would know where and could guess why. It was some consolation to think that if I didn't come home on schedule, my friends would be out here in force to pick up the pieces.

Soon there was no doubt where the signal was coming from, and I changed course for the small yellow star that was dead in line with the beacon. No one, I told myself, would put out a wave this strong unless they had space travel themselves; I might be running into a culture as advanced as my own—with all that that implied.

I was still a long way off when I started calling, not very hopefully, with my own transmitter. To my surprise, there was a prompt reaction. The continuous wave immediately broke up into a string of pulses, repeated over and over again. Even Max couldn't make anything of the message; it probably meant "Who the heck are you?"—which was not a big enough sample for even the most intelligent of translating machines to get its teeth into.

Hour by hour the signal grew in strength; just to let them know I was still around and was reading them loud and clear, I occasionally shot the same message back along the way it had come. And then I had my second big surprise.

I had expected them—whoever or whatever they might be—to switch to speech transmission as soon as I was near enough for good reception. This was precisely what they did; what I had *not* expected was that their voices would be human, the language they spoke an unmistakable but to me unintelligible brand of English. I could identify about one word in ten; the others were either quite unknown or else distorted so badly that I could not recognize them.

When the first words came over the loud-speaker, I guessed the truth. This was no alien, nonhuman race, but something almost as exciting and perhaps a good deal safer as far as a solitary scout was concerned. I had established contact with one of the lost colonies of the First Empire—the pioneers who had set out from Earth in the early days of interstellar exploration, five thousand years ago. When the empire collapsed, most of these isolated groups had perished or had sunk back to barbarism. Here, it seemed, was one that had survived.

I talked back to them in the slowest and simplest English I could muster, but five thousand years is a long time in the life of any language and no real communication was possible. They were clearly excited at the contact—pleasurably, as far as I could judge. This is not always the case; some of the isolated cultures left over from the First Empire have become violently xenophobic and react almost with hysteria to the knowledge that they are not alone in space.

Our attempts to communicate were not making much progress, when a new factor appeared—one that changed my outlook abruptly. A woman's voice started to come from the speaker.

It was the most beautiful voice I'd ever heard, and even without the lonely weeks in space that lay behind me I think I would have fallen in love with it at once. Very deep, yet still completely feminine, it had a warm, caressing quality that seemed to ravish all my senses. I was so stunned, in fact, that it was several minutes before I realized that I could understand what my invisible enchantress was saying. She was speaking English that was almost fifty per cent comprehensible.

To cut a short story shorter, it did not take me very long to learn that her name was Liala, and that she was the only philologist on her planet to specialize in Primitive English. As soon as contact had been made with my ship, she had been called in to do the translating. Luck, it seemed, was very much on my side; the interpreter could so easily have been some ancient, white-bearded fossil.

As the hours ticked away and her sun grew ever larger in the sky ahead of me, Liala and I became the best of friends. Because time was short, I had to operate faster than I'd ever done before. The fact that no one else could understand exactly what we were saying to each other insured our privacy. Indeed, Liala's own knowledge of English was sufficiently imperfect for me to get away with some outrageous remarks; there's no danger of going too far with a girl who'll give you the benefit of the doubt by deciding you couldn't possibly have meant what she thought you said. . . .

Need I say that I felt very, very happy? It looked as if my official and personal interests were neatly coinciding. There was, however, just one slight worry. So far, I had not seen Liala. What if she turned out to be absolutely hideous?

My first chance of settling that important question came six hours from planet-fall. Now I was near enough to pick up video transmissions, and it took Max only a few seconds to analyze the incoming signals and adjust the ship's receiver accordingly. At last I could have my first close-ups of the approaching planet—and of Liala.

She was almost as beautiful as her voice. I stared at the screen, unable to speak, for timeless seconds. Presently she broke the silence. "What's the matter?" she asked. "Haven't you ever seen a girl before?"

I had to admit that I'd seen two or even three, but never one like her. It was a great relief to find that her reaction to me was quite favorable, so it seemed that nothing stood in the way of our future happiness—if we could evade the army of scientists and politicians who would surround me as soon as I landed. Our hopes of privacy were very slender; so much so, in fact, that I felt tempted to break one of my most ironclad rules. I'd even consider *marrying* Liala if that was the only way we could arrange matters. (Yes, that two months in space had really put a strain on my system. . . .)

Five thousand years of history—ten thousand, if you count mine as well—can't be condensed easily into a few hours. But with such a delightful tutor, I absorbed knowledge fast, and everything I missed, Max got down in his infallible memory circuits.

Arcady, as their planet was charmingly called, had been at the very frontier of interstellar colonization; when the tide of empire had retreated, it had been left high and dry. In the struggle to survive, the Arcadians had lost much of their original scientific knowledge, including the secret of the Star Drive. They could not escape from their own solar system, but they had little incentive to do so. Arcady was a fertile world and the low gravity—only a quarter of Earth's—had given the colonists the physical strength they needed to make it live up to its name. Even allowing for any natural bias on Liala's part, it sounded a very attractive place.

Arcady's little yellow sun was already showing a visible disk when I had my brilliant idea. That reception committee had been worrying me, and I suddenly realized how I could keep it at bay. The plan would need Liala's co-operation, but by this time that was assured. If I may say so without sounding too immodest, I have always had a way with women, and this was not my first courtship by TV.

So the Arcadians learned, about two hours before I was due to land, that survey scouts were very shy and suspicious creatures. Owing to previous sad experiences with unfriendly cultures, I politely refused to walk like a fly into their parlor. As there was only one of me, I preferred to meet only one of them, in some isolated spot to be mutually selected. If that meeting went well, I would then fly to the capital city; if not—I'd head back the way I came. I hoped that they would not think this behavior discourteous, but I was a lonely traveler a long way from home, and as reasonable people, I was sure they'd see my point of view. . . .

They did. The choice of the emissary was obvious, and Liala promptly became a world heroine by bravely volunteering to meet the monster from space. She'd radio back, she told her anxious friends, within an hour of coming aboard my ship. I tried to make it two hours, but she said that might be overdoing it, and nasty-minded people might start to talk.

The ship was coming down through the Arcadian atmosphere when I suddenly remembered my compromising pin-ups, and had to make a rapid spring-cleaning. (Even so, one rather explicit masterpiece slipped down behind a chart rack and caused me acute embarrassment when it was discovered by the maintenance crew months later.) When I got back to the control room, the vision screen showed the empty, open plain at the very center of which Liala was waiting for me; in two minutes, I would hold her in my arms, be able to drink the fragrance of her hair, feel her body yield in all the right places—

I didn't bother to watch the landing, for I could rely on Max to do his usual flawless job. Instead, I hurried down to the air lock and waited with what patience I could muster for the opening of the doors that barred me from Liala.

It seemed an age before Max completed the routine air check and gave the "Outer Door Opening" signal. I was through the exit before the metal disk had finished moving, and stood at last on the rich soil of Arcady.

I remembered that I weighed only forty pounds here, so I moved with caution despite my eagerness. Yet I'd forgotten, living in my fool's paradise, what a fractional gravity could do to the human body in the course of two hundred generations. On a small planet, evolution can do a lot in five thousand years.

Liala was waiting for me, and she was as lovely as her picture. There was, however, one trifling matter that the TV screen hadn't told me.

I've never liked big girls, and I like them even less now. If I'd still wanted to, I suppose I could have embraced Liala. But I'd have looked like such a fool, standing there on tiptoe with my arms wrapped around her knees.

# THE STAR

IT IS three thousand light-years to the Vatican. Once, I believed that space could have no power over faith, just as I believed that the heavens declared the glory of God's handiwork. Now I have seen that handiwork, and my faith is sorely troubled. I stare at the crucifix that hangs on the cabin wall above the Mark VI Computer, and for the first time in my life I wonder if it is no more than an empty symbol.

I have told no one yet, but the truth cannot be concealed. The facts are there for all to read, recorded on the countless miles of magnetic tape and the thousands of photographs we are carrying back to Earth. Other scientists can interpret them as easily as I can, and I am not one who would condone that tampering with the truth which often gave my order a bad name in the olden days.

The crew are already sufficiently depressed: I wonder how they will take this ultimate irony. Few of them have any religious faith, yet they will not relish using this final weapon in their campaign against me—that private, good-natured, but fundamentally serious, war which lasted all the way from Earth. It amused them to have a Jesuit as chief astrophysicist: Dr. Chandler, for instance, could never get over it (why are medical men such notorious atheists?). Sometimes he would meet me on the observation deck, where the lights are always low so that the stars shine with undiminished glory. He would come up to me in the gloom and stand staring out of the great oval port, while the heavens crawled slowly

around us as the ship turned end over end with the residual
spin we had never bothered to correct.

"Well, Father," he would say at last, "it goes on forever
and forever, and perhaps *Something* made it. But how you
can believe that Something has a special interest in us and
our miserable little world—that just beats me." Then the
argument would start, while the stars and nebulae would
swing around us in silent, endless arcs beyond the flawlessly
clear plastic of the observation port.

It was, I think, the apparent incongruity of my position
that caused most amusement to the crew. In vain I would
point to my three papers in the *Astrophysical Journal,* my
five in the *Monthly Notices of the Royal Astronomical
Society.* I would remind them that my order has long been
famous for its scientific works. We may be few now, but
ever since the eighteenth century we have made contributions
to astronomy and geophysics out of all proportion to our
numbers. Will my report on the Phoenix Nebula end our
thousand years of history? It will end, I fear, much more
than that.

I do not know who gave the nebula its name, which seems
to me a very bad one. If it contains a prophecy, it is one
that cannot be verified for several billion years. Even the
word nebula is misleading: this is a far smaller object than
those stupendous clouds of mist—the stuff of unborn stars—
that are scattered throughout the length of the Milky Way.
On the cosmic scale, indeed, the Phoenix Nebula is a tiny
thing—a tenuous shell of gas surrounding a single star.

Or what is left of a star . . .

The Rubens engraving of Loyola seems to mock me as it
hangs there above the spectrophotometer tracings. What
would *you,* Father, have made of this knowledge that has
come into my keeping, so far from the little world that was
all the universe you knew? Would your faith have risen to the
challenge, as mine has failed to do?

You gaze into the distance, Father, but I have traveled a
distance beyond any that you could have imagined when you
founded our order a thousand years ago. No other survey
ship has been so far from Earth: we are at the very frontiers
of the explored universe. We set out to reach the Phoenix
Nebula, we succeeded, and we are homeward bound with
our burden of knowledge. I wish I could lift that burden
from my shoulders, but I call to you in vain across the
centuries and the light-years that lie between us.

On the book you are holding the words are plain to read.
AD MAIOREM DEI GLORIAM, the message runs, but it is a mes-

sage I can no longer believe. Would you still believe it, if you could see what we have found?

We knew, of course, what the Phoenix Nebula was. Every year, in our galaxy alone, more than a hundred stars explode, blazing for a few hours or days with thousands of times their normal brilliance before they sink back into death and obscurity. Such are the ordinary novae—the commonplace disasters of the universe. I have recorded the spectrograms and light curves of dozens since I started working at the Lunar Observatory.

But three or four times in every thousand years occurs something beside which even a nova pales into total insignificance.

When a star becomes a *supernova*, it may for a little while outshine all the massed suns of the galaxy. The Chinese astronomers watched this happen in A.D. 1054, not knowing what it was they saw. Five centuries later, in 1572, a supernova blazed in Cassiopeia so brilliantly that it was visible in the daylight sky. There have been three more in the thousand years that have passed since then.

Our mission was to visit the remnants of such a catastrophe, to reconstruct the events that led up to it, and, if possible, to learn its cause. We came slowly in through the concentric shells of gas that had been blasted out six thousand years before, yet were expanding still. They were immensely hot, radiating even now with a fierce violet light, but were far too tenuous to do us any damage. When the star had exploded, its outer layers had been driven upward with such speed that they had escaped completely from its gravitational field. Now they formed a hollow shell large enough to engulf a thousand solar systems, and at its center burned the tiny, fantastic object which the star had now become—a White Dwarf, smaller than the Earth, yet weighing a million times as much.

The glowing gas shells were all around us, banishing the normal night of interstellar space. We were flying into the center of a cosmic bomb that had detonated millennia ago and whose incandescent fragments were still hurtling apart. The immense scale of the explosion, and the fact that the debris already covered a volume of space many billions of miles across, robbed the scene of any visible movement. It would take decades before the unaided eye could detect any motion in these tortured wisps and eddies of gas, yet the sense of turbulent expansion was overwhelming.

We had checked our primary drive hours before, and were drifting slowly toward the fierce little star ahead. Once it had been a sun like our own, but it had squandered in a few hours the energy that should have kept it shining for a million years. Now it was a shrunken miser, hoarding its resources as if trying to make amends for its prodigal youth.

No one seriously expected to find planets. If there had been any before the explosion, they would have been boiled into puffs of vapor, and their substance lost in the greater wreckage of the star itself. But we made the automatic search, as we always do when approaching an unknown sun, and presently we found a single small world circling the star at an immense distance. It must have been the Pluto of this vanished solar system, orbiting on the frontiers of the night. Too far from the central sun ever to have known life, its remoteness had saved it from the fate of all its lost companions.

The passing fires had seared its rocks and burned away the mantle of frozen gas that must have covered it in the days before the disaster. We landed, and we found the Vault.

Its builders had made sure that we should. The monolithic marker that stood above the entrance was now a fused stump, but even the first long-range photographs told us that here was the work of intelligence. A little later we detected the continent-wide pattern of radio-activity that had been buried in the rock. Even if the pylon above the Vault had been destroyed, this would have remained, an immovable and all but eternal beacon calling to the stars. Our ship fell toward this gigantic bull's-eye like an arrow into its target.

The pylon must have been a mile high when it was built, but now it looked like a candle that had melted down into a puddle of wax. It took us a week to drill through the fused rock, since we did not have the proper tools for a task like this. We were astronomers, not archaeologists, but we could improvise. Our original purpose was forgotten: this lonely monument, reared with such labor at the greatest possible distance from the doomed sun, could have only one meaning. A civilization that knew it was about to die had made its last bid for immortality.

It will take us generations to examine all the treasures that were placed in the Vault. They had plenty of time to prepare, for their sun must have given its first warnings many years before the final detonation. Everything that they wished to preserve, all the fruit of their genius, they brought here to this distant world in the days before the end, hoping that some other race would find it and that they would not be utterly forgotten. Would we have done as well, or would we have been too lost in our own misery to give thought to a future we could never see or share?

If only they had had a little more time! They could travel freely enough between the planets of their own sun, but they had not yet learned to cross the interstellar gulfs, and the nearest solar system was a hundred light-years away. Yet even had they possessed the secret of the Transfinite Drive, no more than a few millions could have been saved. Perhaps it was better thus.

Even if they had not been so disturbingly human as their sculpture shows, we could not have helped admiring them and grieving for their fate. They left thousands of visual records and the machines for projecting them, together with elaborate pictorial instructions from which it will not be difficult to learn their written language. We have examined many of these records, and brought to life for the first time in six thousand years the warmth and beauty of a civilization that in many ways must have been superior to our own. Perhaps they only showed us the best, and one can hardly blame them. But their worlds were very lovely, and their cities were built with a grace that matches anything of man's. We have watched them at work and play, and listened to their musical speech sounding across the centuries. One scene is still before my eyes—a group of children on a beach of strange blue sand, playing in the waves as children play on Earth. Curious whiplike trees line the shore, and some very large animal is wading in the shadows yet attracting no attention at all.

And sinking into the sea, still warm and friendly and life-giving, is the sun that will soon turn traitor and obliterate all this innocent happiness.

Perhaps if we had not been so far from home and so vulnerable to loneliness, we should not have been so deeply moved. Many of us had seen the ruins of ancient civilizations on other worlds, but they had never affected us so profoundly. This tragedy was unique. It is one thing for a race to fail and die, as nations and cultures have done on Earth. But to be destroyed so completely in the full flower of its achievement, leaving no survivors—how could that be reconciled with the mercy of God?

My colleagues have asked me that, and I have given what answers I can. Perhaps you could have done better, Father Loyola, but I have found nothing in the *Exercitia Spiritualia* that helps me here. They were not an evil people: I do not know what gods they worshiped, if indeed they worshiped any. But I have looked back at them across the centuries, and have watched while the loveliness they used their last strength to preserve was brought forth again into the light of their shrunken sun. They could have taught us much: why were they destroyed?

I know the answers that my colleagues will give when they get back to Earth. They will say that the universe has no purpose and no plan, that since a hundred suns explode every year in our galaxy, at this very moment some race is dying in the depths of space. Whether that race has done good or evil during its lifetime will make no difference in the end: there is no divine justice, for there is no God.

Yet, of course, what we have seen proves nothing of the sort. Anyone who argues thus is being swayed by emotion, not logic. God has no need to justify His actions to man. He who built the universe can destroy it when He chooses. It is arrogance—it is perilously near blasphemy—for us to say what He may or may not do.

This I could have accepted, hard though it is to look upon whole worlds and peoples thrown into the furnace. But there comes a point when even the deepest faith must falter, and now, as I look at the calculations lying before me, I know I have reached that point at last.

We could not tell, before we reached the nebula, how long ago the explosion took place. Now, from the astronomical evidence and the record in the rocks of that one surviving planet, I have been able to date it very exactly. I know in what year the light of this colossal conflagration reached our Earth. I know how brilliantly the supernova whose corpse now dwindles behind our speeding ship once shone in terrestrial skies. I know how it must have blazed low in the east before sunrise, like a beacon in that oriental dawn.

There can be no reasonable doubt: the ancient mystery is solved at last. Yet, oh God, there were so many stars you could have used. What was the need to give these people to the fire, that the symbol of their passing might shine above Bethlehem?

◎

IF YOU HAVE ONLY LIVED on Earth, you have never seen the sun. Of course, we could not look at it directly, but only through dense filters that cut its rays down to endurable brilliance. It hung there forever above the low, jagged hills to the west of the Observatory, neither rising nor setting, yet moving around a small circle in the sky during the eighty-eight-day year of our little world. For it is not quite true to say that Mercury keeps the same face always turned toward the sun; it wobbles slightly on its axis, and there is a narrow twilight belt which knows such terrestrial commonplaces as dawn and sunset.

We were on the edge of the twilight zone, so that we could take advantage of the cool shadows yet could keep the sun under continuous surveillance as it hovered there above the hills. It was a full-time job for fifty astronomers and other assorted scientists; when we've kept it up for a hundred years or so, we may know something about the small star that brought life to Earth.

There wasn't a single band of solar radiation that someone at the Observatory had not made a life's study and was watching like a hawk. From the far X rays to the longest of radio waves, we had set our traps and snares; as soon as the sun thought of something new, we were ready for it. So we imagined. . . .

The sun's flaming heart beats in a slow, eleven-year rhythm, and we were near the peak of the cycle. Two of the greatest spots ever recorded—each of them large enough to swallow a hundred Earths—had drifted across the disk like great black funnels piercing deeply into the turbulent outer layers of the sun. They were black, of course, only by contrast with the brilliance all around them; even their dark, cool cores were hotter and brighter than an electric arc. We had just watched the second of them disappear around the edge of the disk, wondering if it would survive to reappear two weeks later, when something blew up on the equator.

It was not too spectacular at first, partly because it was almost exactly beneath us—at the precise center of the sun's disk—and so was merged into all the activity around it. If it had been near the edge of the sun, and thus projected against the background of space, it would have been truly awe-inspiring.

Imagine the simultaneous explosion of a million H-bombs. You can't? Nor can anyone else—but that was the sort of thing we were watching climb up toward us at hundreds of miles a second, straight out of the sun's spinning equator. At first it formed a narrow jet, but it was quickly frayed around the edges by the magnetic and gravitational forces that were fighting against it. The central core kept right on, and it was soon obvious that it had escaped from the sun completely and was headed out into space—with us as its first target.

Though this had happened half a dozen times before, it was always exciting. It meant that we could capture some of the very substance of the sun as it went hurtling past in a great cloud of electrified gas. There was no danger; by the time it reached us it would be far too tenuous to do any damage, and, indeed, it would take sensitive instruments to detect it at all.

One of those instruments was the Observatory's radar, which was in continual use to map the invisible ionized layers that surround the sun for millions of miles. This was my department; as soon as there was any hope of picking up the oncoming cloud against the solar background, I aimed my giant radio mirror toward it.

It came in sharp and clear on the long-range screen—a vast, luminous island still moving outward from the sun at hundreds of miles a second. At this distance it was impossible to see its finer details, for my radar waves were taking minutes to make the round trip and to bring me back the information they were presenting on the screen. Even at its speed of not far short of a million miles an hour, it would be almost two days before the escaping prominence reached the orbit of Mercury and swept past us toward the outer planets. But neither Venus nor Earth would record its passing, for they were nowhere near its line of flight.

The hours drifted by; the sun had settled down after the immense convulsion that had shot so many millions of tons of its substance into space, never to return. The aftermath of that eruption was now a slowly twisting and turning cloud a hundred times the size of Earth, and soon it would be close enough for the short-range radar to reveal its finer structure.

Despite all the years I have been in the business, it still gives me a thrill to watch that line of light paint its picture on the screen as it spins in synchronism with the narrow beam of radio waves from the transmitter. I sometimes think of myself as a blind man exploring the space around him with a stick that may be a hundred million miles in length. For man is truly blind to the things I study; these great clouds of ionized gas moving far out from the sun are completely invisible to the eye and even to the most sensitive of photographic plates. They are ghosts that briefly haunt the solar system during the few hours of their existence; if they did not reflect our radar waves or disturb our magnetometers, we should never know that they were there.

The picture on the screen looked not unlike a photograph of a spiral nebula, for as the cloud slowly rotated it trailed ragged arms of gas for ten thousand miles around it. Or it might have been a terrestrial hurricane that I was watching from above as it spun through the atmosphere of Earth. The internal structure was extremely complicated, and was changing minute by minute beneath the action of forces which we have never fully understood. Rivers of fire were flowing in curious paths under what could only be the influence of electric fields; but why were they appearing from nowhere and disappearing again as if matter was being created and destroyed? And what were those gleaming nodules, larger than the moon, that were being swept along like boulders before a flood?

Now it was less than a million miles away; it would be upon us in little more than an hour. The automatic cameras were recording every complete sweep of the radar scan, storing up evidence which was to keep us arguing for years. The magnetic disturbance riding ahead of the cloud had already reached us; indeed, there was hardly an instrument in the Observatory that was not reacting in some way to the onrushing apparition.

I switched to the short-range scanner, and the image of the cloud expanded so enormously that only its central portion was on the screen. At the same time I began to change frequency, tuning across the spectrum to differentiate among the various levels. The shorter the wave length, the farther you can penetrate into a layer of ionized gas; by this technique I hoped to get a kind of X-ray picture of the cloud's interior.

It seemed to change before my eyes as I sliced down through the tenuous outer envelope with its trailing arms, and approached the denser core. "Denser," of course, was a purely relative word; by terrestrial standards even its most closely packed regions were still a fairly good vacuum. I had almost reached the limit of my frequency band, and could shorten the wave length no farther, when I noticed the curious, tight little echo not far from the center of the screen.

It was oval, and much more sharp-edged than the knots of gas we had watched adrift in the cloud's fiery streams. Even in that first glimpse, I knew that here was something very strange and outside all previous records of solar phenomena. I watched it for a dozen scans of the radar beam, then called my assistant away from the radiospectrograph, with which he was analyzing the velocities of the swirling gas as it spun toward us.

"Look, Don," I asked him, "have you ever seen anything like that?"

"No," he answered after a careful examination. "What holds it together? It hasn't changed its shape for the last two minutes."

"That's what puzzles me. Whatever it is, it should have started to break up by now, with all that disturbance going on around it. But it seems as stable as ever."

"How big would you say it is?"

I switched on the calibration grid and took a quick reading. "It's about five hundred miles long, and half that in width."

"Is this the largest picture you can get?"

"I'm afraid so. We'll have to wait until it's closer before we can see what makes it tick."

Don gave a nervous little laugh.

"This is crazy," he said, "but do you know something? I feel as if I'm looking at an amoeba under a microscope."

I did not answer; for, with what I can only describe as a sensation of intellectual vertigo, exactly the same thought had entered my mind.

We forgot about the rest of the cloud, but luckily the automatic cameras kept up their work and no important observations were lost. From now on we had eyes only for that sharp-edged lens of gas that was growing minute by minute as it raced toward us. When it was no farther away than is the moon from Earth, it began to show the first signs of its internal structure, revealing a curious mottled appearance that was never quite the same on two successive sweeps of the scanner.

By now, half the Observatory staff had joined us in the radar room, yet there was complete silence as the oncoming enigma grew swiftly across the screen. It was coming straight toward us; in a few minutes it would hit Mercury somewhere in the center of the daylight side, and that would be the end of it—whatever it was. From the moment we obtained our first really detailed view until the screen became blank again could not have been more than five minutes; for every one of us, that five minutes will haunt us all our lives.

We were looking at what seemed to be a translucent oval, its interior laced with a network of almost invisible lines. Where the lines crossed there appeared to be tiny, pulsing nodes of light; we could never be quite sure of their existence because the radar took almost a minute to paint the complete picture on the screen—and between each sweep the object moved several thousand miles. There was no doubt, however, that the network itself existed; the cameras settled any arguments about that.

So strong was the impression that we were looking at a solid object that I took a few moments off from the radar screen and hastily focused one of the optical telescopes on the sky. Of course, there was nothing to be seen—no sign of anything silhouetted against the sun's pock-marked disk. This was a case where vision failed completely and only the electrical senses of the radar were of any use. The thing that was coming toward us out of the sun was as transparent as air—and far more tenuous.

As those last moments ebbed away, I am quite sure that every one of us had reached the same conclusion—and was waiting for someone to say it first. What we were seeing was impossible, yet the evidence was there before our eyes. We were looking at life, where no life could exist. . . .

The eruption had hurled the thing out of its normal environment, deep down in the flaming atmosphere of the sun. It was a miracle that it had survived its journey through space; already it must be dying, as the forces that controlled its huge, invisible body lost their hold over the electrified gas which was the only substance it possessed.

Today, now that I have run through those films a hundred times, the idea no longer seems so strange to me. For what is life but organized energy? Does it matter *what* form that energy takes—whether it is chemical, as we know it on Earth, or purely electrical, as it seemed to be here? Only the pattern is important; the substance itself is of no significance. But at the time I did not think of this; I was conscious only of a vast and overwhelming wonder as I watched this creature of the sun live out the final moments of its existence.

Was it intelligent? Could it understand the strange doom that had befallen it? There are a thousand such questions that may never be answered. It is hard to see how a creature born in the fires of the sun itself could know anything of the external universe, or could even sense the existence of something as unutterably cold as rigid nongaseous matter. The living island that was falling upon us from space could never have conceived, however intelligent it might be, of the world it was so swiftly approaching.

Now it filled our sky—and perhaps, in those last few seconds, it knew that something strange was ahead of it. It may have sensed the far-flung magnetic field of Mercury, or felt the tug of our little world's gravitational pull. For it had begun to change; the luminous lines that must have been what passed for its nervous system were clumping together in new patterns, and I would have given much to know their meaning. It may be that I was looking into the brain of a mindless beast in its last convulsion of fear—or of a godlike being making its peace with the universe.

Then the radar screen was empty, wiped clean during a single scan of the beam. The creature had fallen below our horizon, and was hidden from us now by the curve of the planet. Far out in the burning dayside of Mercury, in the inferno where only a dozen men have ever ventured and fewer still come back alive, it smashed silently and invisibly against the seas of molten metal, the hills of slowly moving lava. The mere impact could have meant nothing to such an entity; what it could not endure was its first contact with the inconceivable cold of solid matter.

Yes, *cold*. It had descended upon the hottest spot in the solar system, where the temperature never falls below seven hundred degrees Fahrenheit and sometimes approaches a thousand. And that was far, far colder to it than the antarctic winter would be to a naked man.

We did not see it die, out there in the freezing fire; it was beyond the reach of our instruments now, and none of them recorded its end. Yet every one of us knew when that moment came, and that is why we are not interested when those who have seen only the films and tapes tell us that we were watching some purely natural phenomenon.

How can one explain what we felt, in that last moment when half our little world was enmeshed in the dissolving tendrils of that huge but immaterial brain? I can only say that it was a soundless cry of anguish, a death pang that seeped into our minds without passing through the gateways of the senses. Not one of us doubted then, or has ever doubted since, that he had witnessed the passing of a giant.

We may have been both the first and the last of all men to see so mighty a fall. Whatever *they* may be, in their unimaginable world within the sun, our paths and theirs may never cross again. It is hard to see how we can ever make contact wtih them, even if their intelligence matches ours.

And does it? It may be well for us if we never know the answer. Perhaps they have been living there inside the sun since the universe was born, and have climbed to peaks of wisdom that we shall never scale. The future may be theirs, not ours; already they may be talking across the light-years to their cousins in other stars.

One day they may discover us, by whatever strange senses they possess, as we circle around their mighty, ancient home, proud of our knowledge and thinking ourselves lords of creation. They may not like what they find, for to them we should be no more than maggots, crawling upon the skins of worlds too cold to cleanse themselves from the corruption of organic life.

And then, if they have the power, they will do what they consider necessary. The sun will put forth its strength and lick the faces of its children; and thereafter the planets will go their way once more as they were in the beginning—clean and bright. . . . and sterile.

## TRANSIENCE

THE FOREST, which came almost to the edge of the beach, climbed away into the distance up the flanks of the low, misty hills. Underfoot, the sand was coarse and mixed with myriads of broken shells. Here and there the retreating tide had left long streamers of weed trailed across the beach. The rain, which seldom ceased, had for the moment passed inland, but ever and again large, angry drops would beat tiny craters in the sand.

It was hot and sultry, for the war between sun and rain was never-ending. Sometimes the mists would lift for a while and the hills would stand out clearly above the land they guarded. These hills arced in a semicircle along the bay, following the line of the beach, and beyond them could sometimes be seen, at an immense distance, a wall of mountains lying beneath perpetual clouds. The trees grew everywhere, softening the contours of the land so that the hills blended smoothly into each other. Only in one place could the bare, uncovered rock be seen, where long ago some fault had weakened the foundations of the hills, so that for a mile or more the sky line fell sharply away, drooping down to the sea like a broken wing.

Moving with the cautious alertness of a wild animal, the child came through the stunted trees at the forest's edge. For a moment he hesitated; then, since there seemed to be no danger, walked slowly out onto the beach.

He was naked, heavily built, and had coarse black hair tangled over his shoulders. His face, brutish though it was, might almost have passed in human society, but the eyes would have betrayed him. They were not the eyes of an animal, for there was something in their depths that no animal had ever known. But it was no more than a promise. For this child, as for all his race, the light of reason had yet to dawn. Only a hairsbreadth still separated him from the beasts among whom he dwelt.

The tribe had not long since come into this land, and he was the first ever to set foot upon that lonely beach. What had lured him from the known dangers of the forest into the unknown and therefore more terrible dangers of this new element, he could not have told even had he possessed the power of speech. Slowly he walked out to the water's edge, always with backward glances at the forest behind him; and as he did so, for the first time in all history, the level sand bore upon its face the footprints it would one day know so well.

He had met water before, but it had always been bounded and confined by land. Now it stretched endlessly before him, and the sound of its laboring beat ceaselessly upon his ears.

With the timeless patience of the savage, he stood on the moist sand that the water had just relinquished, and as the tide line moved out he followed it slowly, pace by pace. When the waves reached toward his feet with a sudden access of energy, he would retreat a little way toward the land. But something held him here at the water's edge, while his shadow lengthened along the sands and the cold evening wind began to rise around him.

Perhaps into his mind had come something of the wonder of the sea, and a hint of all that it would one day mean to man. Though the first gods of his people still lay far in the future, he felt a dim sense of worship stir within him. He knew that he was now in the presence of something greater than all the powers and forces he had ever met.

The tide was turning. Far away in the forest, a wolf howled once and was suddenly silent. The noises of the night were rising around him, and it was time to go.

Under the low moon, the two lines of footprints interlaced

across the sand. Swiftly the oncoming tide was smoothing them away. But they would return in their thousands and millions, in the centuries yet to be.

The child playing among the rock pools knew nothing of the forest that had once ruled all the land around him. It had left no trace of its existence. As ephemeral as the mists that had so often rolled down from the hills, it, too, had veiled them for a little while and now was gone. In its place had come a checkerboard of fields, the legacy of a thousand years of patient toil. And so the illusion of permanence remained, though everything had altered save the line of the hills against the sky. On the beach, the sand was finer now, and the land had lifted so that the old tide line was far beyond the reach of the questing waves.

Beyond the sea wall and the promenade, the little town was sleeping through the golden summer day. Here and there along the beach, people lay at rest, drowsy with heat and lulled by the murmur of the waves.

Out across the bay, white and gold against the water, a great ship was moving slowly to sea. The boy could hear, faint and far away, the beat of its screws and could still see the tiny figures moving upon its decks and superstructure. To the child—and not to him alone—it was a thing of wonder and beauty. He knew its name and the land to which it was steaming; but he did not know that the splendid ship was both the last and greatest of its kind. He scarcely noticed, almost lost against the glare of the sun, the thin white vapor trails that spelled the doom of the proud and lovely giant.

Soon the great liner was no more than a dark smudge on the horizon, and the boy turned again to his interrupted play, to the tireless building of his battlements of sand. In the west the sun was beginning its long decline, but the evening was still far away.

Yet it came at last, when the tide was returning to the land. At his mother's words, the child gathered up his playthings and, wearily contented, began to follow his parents back to the shore. He glanced once only at the sand castles he had built wth such labor and would not see again. Without regret he left them to the advancing waves, for tomorrow he would return and the future stretched endlessly before him.

That tomorrow would not always come, either for himself or for the world, he was still too young to know.

And now even the hills had changed, worn away by the weight of years. Not all the change was the work of nature,

for one night in the long-forgotten past something had come
sliding down from the stars, and the little town had vanished
in a spinning tower of flame. But that was so long ago that
it was beyond sorrow or regret. Like the fall of fabled Troy
or the overwhelming of Pompeii, it was part of the irre-
mediable past and could rouse no pity now.

On the broken sky line lay a long metal building support-
ing a maze of mirrors that turned and glittered in the sun.
No one from an earlier age could have guessed its purpose.
It was as meaningless as an observatory or a radio station
would have been to ancient man. But it was neither of these
things.

Since noon, Bran had been playing among the shallow
pools left by the retreating tide. He was quite alone, though
the machine that guarded him was watching unobtrusively
from the shore. Only a few days ago, there had been other
children playing beside the blue waters of this lovely bay.
Bran sometimes wondered where they had vanished, but he
was a solitary child and did not greatly care. Lost in his own
dreams, he was content to be left alone.

In the last few hours he had linked the tiny pools with an
intricate network of waterways. His thoughts were very far
from Earth, both in space and time. Around him now were
the dull, red sands of another world. He was Cardenis, prince
of engineers, fighting to save his people from the encroaching
deserts. For Bran had looked upon the ravaged face of Mars;
he knew the story of its long tragedy and the help from Earth
that had come too late.

Out to the horizon the sea was empty, untroubled by ships,
as it had been for ages. For a little while, near the beginning
of time, man had fought his brief war against the oceans of
the world. Now it seemed that only a moment lay between
the coming of the first canoes and the passing of the last
great Megatheria of the seas.

Bran did not even glance at the sky when the monstrous
shadow swept along the beach. For days past, those silver
giants had been rising over the hills in an unending stream,
and now he gave them little thought. All his life he had
watched the great ships climbing through the skies of Earth
on their way to distant worlds. Often he had seen them return
from those long journeys, dropping down through the clouds
with cargoes beyond imagination.

He wondered sometimes why they came no more, those
returning voyagers. All the ships he saw now were outward
bound; never one drove down from the skies to berth at the
great port beyond the hills. Why this should be, no one would

tell him. He had learned not to speak of it now, having seen the sadness that his questions brought.

Across the sands the robot was calling to him softly. "Bran," came the words, echoing the tones of his mother's voice, "Bran—it's time to go."

The child looked up, his face full of indignant denial. He could not believe it. The sun was still high and the tide was far away. Yet along the shore his mother and father were already coming toward him.

They walked swiftly, as though the time were short. Now and again his father would glance for an instant at the sky, then turn his head quickly away as if he knew well that there was nothing he could hope to see. But a moment later he would look again.

Stubborn and angry, Bran stood at bay among his canals and lakes. His mother was strangely silent, but presently his father took him by the hand and said quietly, "You must come with us, Bran. It's time we went."

The child pointed sullenly at the beach. "But it's too early. I haven't finished."

His father's reply held no trace of anger, only a great sadness. "There are many things, Bran, that will not be finished now."

Still uncomprehending, the boy turned to his mother. "Then can I come again tomorrow?"

With a sense of desolating wonder, Bran saw his mother's eyes fill with sudden tears. And he knew at last that never again would he play upon the sands by the azure waters; never again would he feel the tug of the tiny waves about his feet. He had found the sea too late, and now must leave it forever. Out of the future, chilling his soul, came the first faint intimation of the long ages of exile that lay ahead.

He never looked back as they walked silently together across the clinging sand. This moment would be with him all his life, but he was still too stunned to do more than walk blindly into a future he could not understand.

The three figures dwindled into the distance and were gone. A long while later, a silver cloud seemed to lift above the hills and move slowly out to sea. In a shallow arc, as though reluctant to leave its world, the last of the great ships climbed toward the horizon and shrank to nothingness over the edge of the Earth.

The tide was returning with the dying day. As though its makers still walked within its walls, the low metal building upon the hills had begun to blaze with light. Near the zenith, one star had not waited for the sun to set, but already burned with a fierce white glare against the darkling sky. Soon its companions, no longer in the scant thousands that man had once known, began to fill the heavens. The Earth was now near the center of the universe, and whole areas of the sky were an unbroken blaze of light.

But rising beyond the sea in two long curving arms, something black and monstrous eclipsed the stars and seemed to cast its shadow over all the world. The tentacles of the Dark Nebula were already brushing against the frontiers of the solar system. . . .

In the east, a great yellow moon was climbing through the waves. Though man had torn down its mountains and brought it air and water, its face was the one that had looked upon Earth since history began, and it was still the ruler of the tides. Across the sand the line of foam moved steadily onward, overwhelming the little canals and planing down the tangled footprints.

On the sky line, the lights in the strange metal building suddenly died, and the spinning mirrors ceased their moon-light glittering. From far inland came the blinding flash of a great explosion, then another, and another fainter yet.

Presently the ground trembled a little, but no sound disturbed the solitude of the deserted shore.

Under the level light of the sagging moon, beneath the myriad stars, the beach lay waiting for the end. It was alone now, as it had been at the beginning. Only the waves would move, and but for a little while, upon its golden sands.

For Man had come and gone.

# THE SONGS OF DISTANT EARTH

BENEATH THE PALM TREES Lora waited, watching the sea. Clyde's boat was already visible as a tiny notch on the far horizon—the only flaw in the perfect mating of sea and sky. Minute by minute it grew in size, until it had detached itself from the featureless blue globe that encompassed the world. Now she could see Clyde standing at the prow, one hand twined around the rigging, statue-still as his eyes sought her among the shadows.

"Where are you, Lora?" his voice asked plaintively from

the radio bracelet he had given her when they became engaged. "Come and help me—we've got a big catch to bring home."

So! Lora told herself; *that's* why you asked me to hurry down to the beach. Just to punish Clyde and to reduce him to the right state of anxiety, she ignored his call until he had repeated it half a dozen times. Even then she did not press the beautiful golden pearl set in the "Transmit" button, but slowly emerged from the shade of the great trees and walked down the sloping beach.

Clyde looked at her reproachfully, but gave her a satisfactory kiss as soon as he had bounded ashore and secured the boat. Then they started unloading the catch together, scooping fish large and small from both hulls of the catamaran. Lora screwed up her nose but assisted gamely, until the waiting sand sled was piled high with the victims of Clyde's skill.

It was a good catch; when she married Clyde, Lora told herself proudly, she'd never starve. The clumsy, armored creatures of this young planet's sea were not true fish; it would be a hundred million years before nature invented scales here. But they were good enough eating, and the first colonists had labeled them with names they had brought, with so many other traditions, from unforgotten Earth.

"That's the lot!" grunted Clyde, tossing a fair imitation of a salmon onto the glistening heap. "I'll fix the nets later—let's go!"

Finding a foothold with some difficulty, Lora jumped onto the sled behind him. The flexible rollers spun for a moment against the sand, then got a grip. Clyde, Lora, and a hundred pounds of assorted fish started racing up the wave-scalloped beach. They had made half the brief journey when the simple, carefree world they had known all their young lives came suddenly to its end.

The sign of its passing was written there upon the sky, as if a giant hand had drawn a piece of chalk across the blue vault of heaven. Even as Clyde and Lora watched, the gleaming vapor trail began to fray at its edges, breaking up into wisps of cloud.

And now they could hear, falling down through the miles above their heads, a sound their world had not known for generations. Instinctively they grasped each other's hands, as they stared at that snow-white furrow across the sky and listened to the thin scream from the borders of space. The descending ship had already vanished beyond the horizon before they turned to each other and breathed, almost with reverence, the same magic word: "Earth!"

After three hundred years of silence, the mother world had reached out once more to touch Thalassa. . . .

Why? Lora asked herself, when the long moment of revelation had passed and the scream of torn air ceased to echo from the sky. What had happened, after all these years, to bring a ship from mighty Earth to this quiet and contented world? There was no room for more colonists here on this one island in a watery planet, and Earth knew that well enough. Its robot survey ships had mapped and probed Thalassa from space five centuries ago, in the early days of interstellar exploration. Long before man himself had ventured out into the gulfs between the stars, his electronic servants had gone ahead of him, circling the worlds of alien suns and heading homeward with their store of knowledge, as bees bring honey back to the parent hive.

Such a scout had found Thalassa, a freak among worlds with its single large island in a shoreless sea. One day continents would be born here, but this was a new planet, its history still waiting to be written.

The robot had taken a hundred years to make its homeward journey, and for a hundred more its garnered knowledge had slept in the electronic memories of the great computers which stored the wisdom of Earth. The first waves of colonization had not touched Thalassa; there were more profitable worlds to be developed—worlds that were not ninetenths water. Yet at last the pioneers had come; only a dozen miles from where she was standing now, Lora's ancestors had first set foot upon this planet and claimed it for mankind.

They had leveled hills, planted crops, moved rivers, built towns and factories, and multiplied until they reached the natural limits of their land. With its fertile soil, abundant seas, and mild, wholly predictable weather, Thalassa was not a world that demanded much of its adopted children. The pioneering spirit had lasted perhaps two generations; thereafter the colonists were content to work as much as necessary (but no more), to dream nostalgically of Earth, and to let the future look after itself.

The village was seething with speculation when Clyde and Lora arrived. News had already come from the northern end of the island that the ship had spent its furious speed and was heading back at a low altitude, obviously looking for a place to land. "They'll still have the old maps," someone said. "Ten to one they'll ground where the first expedition landed, up in the hills."

It was a shrewd guess, and within minutes all available transport was moving out of the village, along the seldom-used road to the west. As befitted the mayor of so important a cultural center as Palm Bay (population: 572; occupations: fishing, hydroponics; industries: none), Lora's father led the way in his official car. The fact that its annual coat of paint was just about due was perhaps a little unfortunate; one could only hope that the visitors would overlook the occasional patches of bare metal. After all, the car itself was quite new; Lora could distinctly remember the excitement its arrival had caused, only thirteen years ago.

The little caravan of assorted cars, trucks, and even a couple of straining sand sleds rolled over the crest of the hill and ground to a halt beside the weathered sign with its simple but impressive words:

LANDING SITE OF THE FIRST EXPEDITION TO THALASSA
1 JANUARY, YEAR ZERO
(28 May A.D. 2626)

The *first* expedition, Lora repeated silently. There had never been a second one—*but here it was. . . .*

The ship came in so low, and so silently, that it was almost upon them before they were aware of it. There was no sound of engines—only a brief rustling of leaves as the displaced air stirred among the trees. Then all was still once more, but it seemed to Lora that the shining ovoid resting on the turf was a great silver egg, waiting to hatch and to bring something new and strange into the peaceful world of Thalassa.

"It's so small," someone whispered behind her. "They couldn't have come from Earth in *that* thing!"

"Of course not," the inevitable self-appointed expert replied at once. "That's only a lifeboat—the real ship's up there in space. Don't you remember that the first expedition—"

"Sshh!" someone else remonstrated. "They're coming out!"

It happened in the space of a single heartbeat. One second the seamless hull was so smooth and unbroken that the eye looked in vain for any sign of an opening. And then, an instant later, there was an oval doorway with a short ramp leading to the ground. Nothing had moved, but something had *happened*. How it had been done, Lora could not imagine, but she accepted the miracle without surprise. Such things were only to be expected of a ship that came from Earth.

There were figures moving inside the shadowed entrance;

not a sound came from the waiting crowd as the visitors
slowly emerged and stood blinking in the fierce light of an
unfamiliar sun. There were seven of them—all men—and
they did not look in the least like the super-beings she had
expected. It was true that they were all somewhat above the
average in height and had thin, clear-cut features, but they
were so pale that their skins were almost white. They seemed,
moreover, worried and uncertain, which was something that
puzzled Lora very much. For the first time it occurred to her
that this landing on Thalassa might be unintentional, and that
the visitors were as surprised to be here as the islanders were
to greet them.

The mayor of Palm Bay, confronted with the supreme
moment of his career, stepped forward to deliver the speech
on which he had been frantically working ever since the car
left the village. A second before he opened his mouth, a
sudden doubt struck him and sponged his memory clean.
Everyone had automatically assumed that this ship came
from Earth—but that was pure guesswork. It might just as
easily have been sent here from one of the other colonies, of
which there were at least a dozen much closer than the
parent world. In his panic over protocol, all that Lora's father
could manage was: "We welcome you to Thalassa. You're
from Earth—I presume?" That "I presume?" was to make
Mayor Fordyce immortal; it would be a century before
anyone discovered that the phrase was not quite original.

In all that waiting crowd, Lora was the only one who
never heard the confirming answer, spoken in English that
seemed to have speeded up a trifle during the centuries of
separation. For in that moment, she saw Leon for the first
time.

He came out of the ship, moving as unobtrusively as possible to join his companions at the foot of the ramp. Perhaps
he had remained behind to make some adjustment to the
controls; perhaps—and this seemed more likely—he had been
reporting the progress of the meeting to the great mother
ship, which must be hanging up there in space, far beyond
the uttermost fringes of the atmosphere. Whatever the
reason, from then onward Lora had eyes for no one else.

Even in that first instant, she knew that her life could
never again be the same. This was something new and beyond
all her experience, filling her at the same moment with
wonder and fear. Her fear was for the love she felt for
Clyde; her wonder for the new and unknown thing that had
come into her life.

Leon was not as tall as his companions, but was much

more stockily built, giving an impression of power and competence. His eyes, very dark and full of animation, were deep-set in rough-hewn features which no one could have called handsome, yet which Lora found disturbingly attractive. Here was a man who had looked upon sights she could not imagine—a man who, perhaps, had walked the streets of Earth and seen its fabled cities. What was he doing here on lonely Thalassa, and why were those lines of strain and worry about his ceaselessly searching eyes?

He had looked at her once already, but his gaze had swept on without faltering. Now it came back, as if prompted by memory, and for the first time he became conscious of Lora, as all along she had been aware of him. Their eyes locked, bridging gulfs of time and space and experience. The anxious furrows faded from Leon's brow, the tense lines slowly relaxed; and presently he smiled.

It was dusk when the speeches, the banquets, the receptions, the interviews were over. Leon was very tired, but his mind was far too active to allow him to sleep. After the strain of the last few weeks, when he had awakened to the shrill clamor of alarms and fought with his colleagues to save the wounded ship, it was hard to realize that they had reached safety at last. What incredible good fortune that this inhabited planet had been so close! Even if they could not repair the ship and complete the two centuries of flight that still lay before them, here at least they could remain among friends. No shipwrecked mariners, of sea or space, could hope for more than that.

The night was cool and calm, and ablaze with unfamiliar stars. Yet there were still some old friends, even though the ancient patterns of the constellations were hopelessly lost. There was mighty Rigel, no fainter for all the added light-years that its rays must now cross before they reached his eyes. And that must be giant Canopus, almost in line with their destination, but so much more remote that even when they reached their new home, it would seem no brighter than in the skies of Earth.

Leon shook his head, as if to clear the stupefying, hypnotic image of immensity from his mind. Forget the stars, he told himself; you will face them again soon enough. Cling to this little world while you are upon it, even though it may be a grain of dust on the road between the Earth you will never see again and the goal that waits for you at journey's end, two hundred years from now.

His friends were already sleeping, tired and content, as

they had a right to be. Soon he would join them—when his restless spirit would allow him to. But first he would see something of this world to which chance had brought him, this oasis peopled by his own kinsmen in the deserts of space.

He left the long, single-storied guesthouse that had been prepared for them in such obvious haste, and walked out into the single street of Palm Bay. There was no one about, though sleepy music came from a few houses. It seemed that the villagers believed in going to bed early—or perhaps they, too, were exhausted by the excitement and hospitality of the day. That suited Leon, who wanted only to be left alone until his racing thoughts had slowed to rest.

Out of the quiet night around him he became aware of the murmuring sea, and the sound drew his footsteps away from the empty street. It was dark among the palms, when the lights of the village had faded behind him, but the smaller of Thalassa's two moons was high in the south and its curious yellow glow gave him all the guidance he required. Presently he was through the narrow belt of trees, and there at the end of the steeply shelving beach lay the ocean that covered almost all of this world.

A line of fishing boats was drawn up at the water's edge, and Leon walked slowly toward them, curious to see how the craftsmen of Thalassa had solved one of man's oldest problems. He looked approvingly at the trim plastic hulls, the narrow outrigger float, the power-operated winch for raising the nets, the compact little motor, the radio with its direction-finding loop. This almost primitive, yet completely adequate, simplicity had a profound appeal to him; it was hard to think of a greater contrast with the labyrinthine complexities of the mighty ship hanging up there above his head. For a moment he amused himself with fantasy; how pleasant to jettison all his years of training and study, and to exchange the life of a starship propulsion engineer for the peaceful, undemanding existence of a fisherman! They must need someone to keep their boats in order, and perhaps he could think of a few improvements. . . .

He shrugged away the rosy dream, without bothering to marshal all its obvious fallacies, and began to walk along the shifting line of foam where the waves had spent their last strength against the land. Underfoot was the debris of this young ocean's newborn life—empty shells and carapaces that might have littered the coasts of Earth a billion years ago. Here, for instance, was a tightly wound spiral of limestone which he had surely seen before in some museum. It might well be; any design that had once served her purpose, Nature repeated endlessly on world after world.

A faint yellow glow was spreading swiftly across the eastern sky; even as Leon watched, Selene, the inner moon, edged itself above the horizon. With astonishing speed, the entire gibbous disk climbed out of the sea, flooding the beach with sudden light.

And in that burst of brilliance, Leon saw that he was not alone.

The girl was sitting on one of the boats, about fifty yards farther along the beach. Her back was turned toward him and she was staring out to sea, apparently unaware of his presence. Leon hesitated, not wishing to invade her solitude, and also being uncertain of the local mores in these matters. It seemed highly likely, at such a time and place, that she was waiting for someone; it might be safest, and most tactful, to turn quietly back to the village.

He had decided too late. As if startled by the flood of new light along the beach, the girl looked up and at once caught sight of him. She rose to her feet with an unhurried grace, showing no signs of alarm or annoyance. Indeed, if Leon could have seen her face clearly in the moonlight, he would have been surprised at the quiet satisfaction it expressed.

Only twelve hours ago, Lora would have been indignant had anyone suggested that she would meet a complete stranger here on this lonely beach when the rest of her world was slumbering. Even now, she might have tried to rationalize her behavior, to argue that she felt restless and could not sleep, and had therefore decided to go for a walk. But she knew in her heart that this was not the truth; all day long she had been haunted by the image of that young engineer, whose name and position she had managed to discover without, she hoped, arousing too much curiosity among her friends.

It was not even luck that she had seen him leave the guesthouse; she had been watching most of the evening from the porch of her father's residence, on the other side of the street. And it was certainly not luck, but deliberate and careful planning, that had taken her to this point on the beach as soon as she was sure of the direction Leon was heading.

He came to a halt a dozen feet away. (Did he recognize her? Did he guess that this was no accident? For a moment her courage almost failed her, but it was too late now to retreat.) Then he gave a curious, twisted smile that seemed to light up his whole face and made him look even younger than he was.

"Hello," he said. "I never expected to meet anyone at this time of night. I hope I haven't disturbed you."

"Of course not," Lora answered, trying to keep her voice as steady and emotionless as she could.

"I'm from the ship, you know. I thought I'd have a look at Thalassa while I'm here."

At those last words, a sudden change of expression crossed Lora's face; the sadness he saw there puzzled Leon, for it could have no cause. And then, with an instantaneous shock of recognition, he knew that he had seen this girl before, and understood what she was doing here. This was the girl who had smiled at him when he came out of the ship—no, that was not right; *he* had been the one who smiled. . . .

There seemed nothing to say. They stared at each other across the wrinkled sand, each wondering at the miracle that had brought them together out of the immensity of time and space. Then, as if in unconscious agreement, they sat facing each other on the gunwale of the boat, still without a word.

This is folly, Leon told himself. What am I doing here? What right have I, a wanderer passing through this world, to touch the lives of its people? I should make my apologies and leave this girl to the beach and the sea that are her birthright, not mine.

Yet he did not leave. The bright disk of Selene had risen a full hand's breadth above the sea when he said at last: "What's your name?"

"I'm Lora," she answered, in the soft, lilting accent of the islanders, which was so attractive, but not always easy to understand.

"And I'm Leon Carrell, Assistant Propulsion Engineer, Starship *Magellan*."

She gave a little smile as he introduced himself, and at that moment Leon was certain that she already knew his name. At the same time a completely irrelevant and whimsical thought struck him; until a few minutes ago he had been dead-tired, just about to turn back for his overdue sleep. Yet now he was fully awake and alert—poised, as it were, on the brink of a new and unpredictable adventure.

But Lora's next remark was predictable enough: "How do you like Thalassa?"

"Give me time," Leon countered. "I've only seen Palm Bay, and not much of that."

"Will you be here—very long?"

The pause was barely perceptible, but his ear detected it. *This* was the question that really mattered.

"I'm not sure," he replied, truthfully enough. "It depends on how long the repairs take."

"What went wrong?"

"Oh, we ran into something too big for our meteor screen to absorb. And—bang!—that was the end of the screen. So we've got to make a new one."

"And you think you can do that here?"

"We hope so. The main problem will be lifting about a million tons of water up to the *Magellan*. Luckily, I think Thalassa can spare it."

"Water? I don't understand."

"Well, you know that a starship travels at almost the speed of light; even then it takes years to get anywhere, so that we have to go into suspended animation and let the automatic controls run the ship."

Lora nodded. "Of course—that's how our ancestors got here."

"Well, the speed would be no problem if space was really empty—but it isn't. A starship sweeps up thousands of atoms of hydrogen, particles of dust, and sometimes larger fragments, every second of its flight. At nearly the speed of light, these bits of cosmic junk have enormous energy, and could soon burn up the ship. So we carry a shield about a mile ahead of us, and let *that* get burned up instead. Do you have umbrellas on this world?"

"Why—yes," Lora replied, obviously baffled by the incongruous question.

"Then you can compare a starship to a man moving head down through a rainstorm behind the cover of an umbrella. The rain is the cosmic dust between the stars, and our ship was unlucky enough to lose its umbrella."

"And you can make a new one of *water*?"

"Yes; it's the cheapest building material in the universe. We freeze it into an iceberg which travels ahead of us. What could be simpler than that?"

Lora did not answer; her thoughts seemed to have veered onto a new track. Presently she said, her voice so low and wistful that Leon had to bend forward to hear it against the rolling of the surf: "And you left Earth a hundred years ago."

"A hundred and four. Of course, it seems only a few weeks, since we were deep-sleeping until the autopilot revived us. All the colonists are still in suspended animation; they don't know that anything's happened."

"And presently you'll join them again, and sleep your way on to the stars."

Leon nodded, avoiding her eye. "That's right. Planetfall will be a few months late, but what does that matter on a trip that takes three hundred years?"

Lora pointed to the island behind them, and then to the shoreless sea at whose edge they stood.

"It's strange to think that your sleeping friends up there will never know anything of all this. I feel sorry for them."

"Yes, only we fifty or so engineers will have any memories of Thalassa. To everyone else in the ship, our stop here will be nothing more than a hundred-year-old entry in the log-book."

He glanced at Lora's face, and saw again that sadness in her eyes.

"Why does that make you unhappy?"

She shook her head, unable to answer. How could one express the sense of loneliness that Leon's words had brought to her? The lives of men, and all their hopes and fears, were so little against the inconceivable immensities that they had dared to challenge. The thought of that three-hundred-year journey, not yet half completed, was something from which her mind recoiled in horror. And yet—in her own veins was the blood of those earlier pioneers who had followed the same path to Thalassa, centuries ago.

The night was no longer friendly; she felt a sudden longing for her home and family, for the little room that held everything she owned and that was all the world she knew or wanted. The cold of space was freezing her heart; she wished now that she had never come on this mad adventure. It was time—more than time—to leave.

As she rose to her feet, she noticed that they had been sitting on Clyde's boat, and wondered what unconscious prompting of her mind had brought her here to this one vessel out of all the little fleet lined up along the beach. At the thought of Clyde, a spasm of uncertainty, even of guilt, swept over her. Never in her life, except for the most fleeting moments, had she thought of any other man but him. Now she could no longer pretend that this was true.

"What's the matter?" asked Leon. "Are you cold?" He held out his hand to her, and for the first time their fingers touched as she automatically responded. But at the instant of contact, she shied like a startled animal and jerked away.

"I'm all right," she answered, almost angrily. "It's late—I must go home. Good-by."

Her reaction was so abrupt that it took Leon by surprise. Had he said anything to offend her? he wondered. She was already walking quickly away when he called after her: "Will I see you again?"

If she answered, the sound of the waves carried away her voice. He watched her go, puzzled and a little hurt, while not for the first time in his life he reflected how hard it was to understand the mind of a woman.

For a moment he thought of following her and repeating the question, but in his heart he knew there was no need. As surely as the sun would rise tomorrow, they would meet again.

And now the life of the island was dominated by the crippled giant a thousand miles out in space. Before dawn and after sunset, when the world was in darkness but the light of the sun still streamed overhead, the *Magellan* was visible as a brilliant star, the brightest object in all the sky except the two moons themselves. But even when it could not be seen—when it was lost in the glare of day or eclipsed by the shadow of Thalassa—it was never far from men's thoughts.

It was hard to believe that only fifty of the starship's crew had been awakened, and that not even half of those were on Thalassa at any one time. They seemed to be everywhere, usually in little groups of two or three, walking swiftly on mysterious errands or riding small antigravity scooters which floated a few feet from the ground and moved so silently that they made life in the village rather hazardous. Despite the most pressing invitations, the visitors had still taken no part in the cultural and social activities of the island. They had explained, politely but firmly, that until the safety of their ship was secured, they would have no time for any other interests. Later, certainly, but not now . . .

So Thalassa had to wait with what patience it could muster while the Earthmen set up their instruments, made their surveys, drilled deep into the rocks of the island, and carried out scores of experiments which seemed to have no possible connection with their problem. Sometimes they consulted briefly with Thalassa's own scientists, but on the whole they kept to themselves. It was not that they were unfriendly or aloof; they were working with such a fierce and dedicated intensity that they were scarcely aware of anyone around them.

After their first meeting, it was two days before Lora spoke to Leon again. She saw him from time to time as he hurried about the village, usually with a bulging brief case and an abstracted expression, but they were able to exchange only the briefest of smiles. Yet even this was enough to keep her emotions in turmoil, to banish her peace of mind, and to poison her relationship with Clyde.

As long as she could remember, he had been part of her life; they had had their quarrels and disagreements, but no one else had ever challenged his place in her heart. In a few months they would be married—yet now she was not even sure of that, or indeed of anything.

"Infatuation" was an ugly word, which one applied only to other people. But how else could she explain this yearning to be with a man who had come suddenly into her life from nowhere, and who must leave again in a few days or weeks? No doubt the glamour and romance of his origin was partly responsible, but that alone was not enough to account for it. There were other Earthmen better looking than Leon, yet she had eyes for him alone, and her life now was empty unless she was in his presence.

By the end of the first day, only her family knew about her feelings; by the end of the second, everyone she passed gave her a knowing smile. It was impossible to keep a secret in such a tight and talkative community as Palm Bay, and she knew better than to attempt it.

Her second meeting with Leon was accidental—as far as such things can ever be accidents. She was helping her father deal with some of the correspondence and inquiries that had flooded upon the village since the Earthmen's arrival, and was trying to make some sense out of her notes when the door of the office opened. It had opened so often in the last few days that she had ceased to look up; her younger sister was acting as receptionist and dealt with all the visitors. Then she heard Leon's voice; and the paper blurred before her eyes, the notes might have been in an unknown language.

"Can I see the mayor, please?"

"Of course, Mr.—?"

"Assistant Engineer Carrell."

"I'll go and fetch him. Won't you sit down?"

Leon slumped wearily on the ancient armchair that was the best the reception room could offer its infrequent visitors, and not until then did he notice that Lora was watching him silently from the other side of the room. At once he sloughed off his tiredness and shot to his feet.

"Hello—I didn't know you worked here."

"I live here; my father's the mayor."

This portentous news did not seem to impress Leon unduly. He walked over to the desk and picked up the fat volume through which Lora had been browsing between her secretarial duties.

*"A Concise History of Earth,"* he read, *"from the Dawn of Civilization to the Beginning of Interstellar Flight.* And all in a thousand pages! It's a pity it ends three hundred years ago."

"We hope that you'll soon bring us up to date. Has much happened since that was written?"

"Enough to fill about fifty libraries, I suppose. But before we go we'll leave you copies of all our records, so that your history books will only be a hundred years out of date."

They were circling around each other, avoiding the only thing that was important. *When can we meet again?* Lora's thoughts kept hammering silently, unable to break through the barrier of speech. *And does he really like me or is he merely making polite conversation?*

The inner door opened, and the mayor emerged apologetically from his office.

"Sorry to keep you waiting, Mr. Carrell, but the president was on the line—he's coming over this afternoon. And what can I do for you?"

Lora pretended to work, but she typed the same sentence eight times while Leon delivered his message from the captain of the *Magellan.* She was not a great deal wiser when he had finished; it seemed that the starship's engineers wished to build some equipment on a headland a mile from the village, and wanted to make sure there would be no objection.

"Of course!" said Mayor Fordyce expansively, in his nothing's-too-good-for-our-guests tone of voice. "Go right ahead—the land doesn't belong to anybody, and no one lives there. What do you want to do with it?"

"We're building a gravity inverter, and the generator has to be anchored in solid bedrock. It may be a little noisy when it starts to run, but I don't think it will disturb you here in the village. And of course we'll dismantle the equipment when we've finished."

Lora had to admire her father. She knew perfectly well that Leon's request was as meaningless to him as it was to her, but one would never have guessed it.

"That's perfectly all right—glad to be of any help we can. And will you tell Captain Gold that the president's coming at five this afternoon? I'll send my car to collect him; the reception's at five thirty in the village hall."

When Leon had given his thanks and departed, Mayor Fordyce walked over to his daughter and picked up the slim pile of correspondence she had none-too-accurately typed.

"He seems a pleasant young man," he said, "but is it a good idea to get too fond of him?"

"I don't know what you mean."

"Now, Lora! After all, I *am* your father, and I'm not *completely* unobservant."

"He's not"—sniff—"a bit interested in me."

"Are you interested in him?"

"I don't know. Oh, Daddy, I'm so unhappy!"

Mayor Fordyce was not a brave man, so there was only one thing he could do. He donated his handkerchief, and fled back into his office.

It was the most difficult problem that Clyde had ever faced in his life, and there were no precedents that gave any help at all. Lora belonged to him—everyone knew that. If his rival had been another villager, or someone from any other part of Thalassa, he knew exactly what he would have done. But the laws of hospitality, and, above all, his natural awe for anything of Earth, prevented him from politely asking Leon to take his attentions elsewhere. It would not be the first time *that* had happened, and there had never been the slightest trouble on those earlier occasions. That could have been because Clyde was over six feet tall, proportionally broad, and had no excess fat on his one hundred and ninety-pound frame.

During the long hours at sea, when he had nothing else to do but to brood, Clyde toyed with the idea of a short, sharp bout with Leon. It would be very short; though Leon was not as skinny as most of the Earthmen, he shared their pale, washed-out look and was obviously no match for anyone who led a life of physical activity. That was the trouble—it wouldn't be fair. Clyde knew that public opinion would be outraged if he had a fight with Leon, however justified he might be.

And how justified was he? That was the big problem that worried Clyde, as it had worried a good many billion men before him. It seemed that Leon was now practically one of the family; every time he called at the mayor's house, the Earthman seemed to be there on some pretext or other. Jealousy was an emotion that had never afflicted Clyde before, and he did not enjoy the symptoms.

He was still furious about the dance. It had been the biggest social event for years; indeed, it was not likely that Palm Bay would ever match it again in the whole of its history. To have the president of Thalassa, half the council, and fifty visitors from Earth in the village at the same moment was not something that could happen again this side of eternity.

For all his size and strength, Clyde was a good dancer

—especially with Lora. But that night he had had little chance of proving it; Leon had been too busy demonstrating the latest steps from Earth (latest, that is, if you overlooked the fact that they must have passed out of fashion a hundred years ago—unless they had come back and were now the latest thing). In Clyde's opinion Leon's technique was very poor and the dances were ugly; the interest that Lora showed in them was perfectly ridiculous.

He had been foolish enough to tell her so when his opportunity came; and that had been the last dance he had had with Lora that evening. From then onward, he might not have been there, as far as she was concerned. Clyde had endured the boycott as long as he could, then had left for the bar with one objective in mind. He had quickly attained it, and not until he had come reluctantly to his senses the next morning did he discover what he had missed.

The dancing had ended early; there had been a short speech from the president—his third that evening—introducing the commander of the starship and promising a little surprise. Captain Gold had been equally brief; he was obviously a man more accustomed to orders than orations.

"Friends," he began, "you know why we're here, and I've no need to say how much we appreciate your hospitality and kindness. We shall never forget you, and we're only sorry that we have had so little time to see more of your beautiful island and its people. I hope you will forgive us for any seeming discourtesy, but the repair of our ship, and the safety of our companions, has had to take priority in our minds.

"In the long run, the accident that brought us here may be fortunate for us both. It has given us happy memories, and also inspiration. What we have seen here is a lesson to us. May we make the world that is waiting at the end of our journey as fair a home for mankind as you have made Thalassa.

"And before we resume our voyage, it is both a duty and a pleasure to leave with you all the records we can that will bridge the gap since you last had contact with Earth. Tomorrow we shall invite your scientists and historians up to our ship so that they can copy any of our information tapes they desire. Thus we hope to leave you a legacy which will enrich your world for generations to come. That is the very least we can do.

"But tonight, science and history can wait, for we have other treasures aboard. Earth has not been idle in the centuries since your forefathers left. Listen, now, to some of the heritage we share together, and which we will leave upon Thalassa before we go our way."

The lights had dimmed; the music had begun. No one who was present would ever forget that moment; in a trance of wonder, Lora had listened to what men had wrought in sound during the centuries of separation. Time had meant nothing; she had not even been conscious of Leon standing by her side, holding her hand, as the music ebbed and flowed around them.

These were the things that she had never known, the things that belonged to Earth, and to Earth alone. The slow beat of mighty bells, climbing like invisible smoke from old cathedral spires; the chant of patient boatmen, in a thousand tongues now lost forever, rowing home against the tide in the last light of day; the songs of armies marching into battles that time had robbed of all their pain and evil; the merged murmur of ten million voices as man's greatest cities woke to meet the dawn; the cold dance of the Aurora over endless seas of ice; the roar of mighty engines climbing upward on the highway to the stars. All these she had heard in the music and the songs that had come out of the night—the songs of distant Earth, carried to her across the light-years. . . .

A clear soprano voice, swooping and soaring like a bird at the very edge of hearing, sang a wordless lament that tore at the heart. It was a dirge for all loves lost in the loneliness of space, for friends and homes that could never again be seen and must fade at last from memory. It was a song for all exiles, and it spoke as clearly to those who were sundered from Earth by a dozen generations as to the voyagers to whom its fields and cities still seemed only weeks away.

The music had died into the darkness; misty-eyed, avoiding words, the people of Thalassa had gone slowly to their homes. But Lora had not gone to hers; against the loneliness that had pierced her very soul, there was only one defense. And presently she had found it, in the warm night of the forest, as Leon's arms tightened around her and their souls and bodies merged. Like wayfarers lost in a hostile wilderness, they had sought warmth and comfort beside the fire of love. While that fire burned, they were safe from the shadows that prowled in the night; and all the universe of stars and planets shrank to a toy that they could hold within their hands.

To Leon, it was never wholly real. Despite all the urgency and peril that had brought them here, he sometimes fancied that at journey's end it would be hard to convince himself that Thalassa was not a dream that had come in his long sleep.

This fierce and foredoomed love, for example; he had not asked for it—it had been thrust upon him. Yet there were few men, he told himself, who would not have taken it, had they, too, landed, after weeks of grinding anxiety, on this peaceful, pleasant world.

When he could escape from work, he took long walks with Lora in the fields far from the village, where men seldom came and only the robot cultivators disturbed the solitude. For hours Lora would question him about Earth—but she would never speak of the planet that was the *Magellan*'s goal. He understood her reasons well enough, and did his best to satisfy her endless curiosity about the world that was already "home" to more men than had ever seen it with their own eyes.

She was bitterly disappointed to hear that the age of cities had passed. Despite all that Leon could tell her about the completely decentralized culture that now covered the planet from pole to pole, she still thought of Earth in terms of such vanished giants as Chandrigar, London, Astrograd, New York, and it was hard for her to realize that they had gone forever, and with them the way of life they represented.

"When we left Earth," Leon explained, "the largest centers of population were university towns like Oxford or Ann Arbor or Canberra; some of them had fifty thousand students and professors. There are no other cities left of even half that size."

"But what happened to them?"

"Oh, there was no single cause, but the development of communications started it. As soon as anyone on Earth could see and talk to anyone else by pressing a button, most of the need for cities vanished. Then antigravity was invented, and you could move goods or houses or anything else through the sky without bothering about geography. *That* completed the job of wiping out distance, which the airplane had begun a couple of centuries earlier. After that, men started to live where they liked, and the cities dwindled away."

For a moment Lora did not answer; she was lying on a bank of grass, watching the behavior of a bee whose ancestors, like hers, had been citizens of Earth. It was trying vainly to extract nectar from one of Thalassa's native flowers; insect life had not yet arisen on this world, and the few indigenous flowers had not yet invented lures for air-borne visitors.

The frustrated bee gave up the hopeless task and buzzed angrily away; Lora hoped that it would have enough sense to head back to the orchards, where it would find more co-operative flowers. When she spoke again, it was to voice a dream that had now haunted mankind for almost a thousand years.

"Do you suppose," she said wistfully, "that we'll ever break through the speed of light?"

Leon smiled, knowing where her thoughts were leading. To travel faster than light—to go home to Earth, yet to return to your native world while your friends were still alive—every colonist must, at some time or other, have dreamed of this. There was no problem, in the whole history of the human race, that had called forth so much effort and that still remained so utterly intractable.

"I don't believe so," he said. "If it could be done, someone would have discovered how by this time. No—we have to do it the slow way, because there isn't any other. That's how the universe is built, and there's nothing we can do about it."

"But surely we could still keep in touch!"

Leon nodded. "That's true," he said, "and we try to. I don't know what's gone wrong, but you should have heard from Earth long before now. We've been sending out robot message carriers to all the colonies, carrying a full history of everything that's happened up to the time of departure, and asking for a report back. As the news returns to Earth, it's all transcribed and sent out again by the next messenger. So we have a kind of interstellar news service, with the Earth as the central clearinghouse. It's slow, of course, but there's no other way of doing it. If the last messenger to Thalassa has been lost, there must be another on the way—maybe several, twenty or thirty years apart."

Lora tried to envisage the vast, star-spanning network of message carriers, shuttling back and forth between Earth and its scattered children, and wondered why Thalassa had been overlooked. But with Leon beside her, it did not seem important. He was here; Earth and the stars were very far away. And so also, with whatever unhappiness it might bring, was tomorrow. . . .

By the end of the week, the visitors had built a squat and heavily braced pyramid of metal girders, housing some obscure mechanism, on a rocky headland overlooking the sea. Lora, in common with the 571 other inhabitants of Palm Bay and the several thousand sight-seers who had descended upon the village, was watching when the first test was made. No one was allowed to go within a quarter of a mile of the machine— a precaution that aroused a good deal of alarm among the more nervous islanders. Did the Earthmen know what they were doing? Suppose that something went wrong. And *what* were they doing, anyway?

Leon was there with his friends inside that metal pyramid, making the final adjustments—the "coarse focusing," he had told Lora, leaving her none the wiser. She watched with the same anxious incomprehension as all her fellow islanders until the distant figures emerged from the machine and walked to the edge of the flat-topped rock on which it was built. There they stood, a tiny group of figures silhouetted against the ocean, staring out to sea.

A mile from the shore, something strange was happening to the water. It seemed that a storm was brewing—but a storm that kept within an area only a few hundred yards across. Mountainous waves were building up, smashing against each other and then swiftly subsiding again. Within a few minutes the ripples of the disturbance had reached the shore, but the center of the tiny storm showed no sign of movement. It was as if, Lora told herself, an invisible finger had reached down from the sky and was stirring the sea.

Quite abruptly, the entire pattern changed. Now the waves were no longer battering against each other; they were marching in step, moving more and more swiftly in a tight circle. A cone of water was rising from the sea, becoming taller and thinner with every second. Already it was a hundred feet high, and the sound of its birth was an angry roaring that filled the air and struck terror into the hearts of all who heard it. All, that is, except the little band of men who had summoned this monster from the deep, and who still stood watching it with calm assurance, ignoring the waves that were breaking almost against their feet.

Now the spinning tower of water was climbing swiftly up the sky, piercing the clouds like an arrow as it headed toward space. Its foam-capped summit was already lost beyond sight, and from the sky there began to fall a steady shower of rain, the drops abnormally large, like those which prelude a thunderstorm. Not all the water that was being lifted from Thalassa's single ocean was reaching its distant goal; some was escaping from the power that controlled it and was falling back from the edge of space.

Slowly the watching crowd drifted away, astonishment and fright already yielding to a calm acceptance. Man had been able to control gravity for half a thousand years, and this trick—spectacular though it was—could not be compared with the miracle of hurling a great starship from sun to sun at little short of the speed of light.

The Earthmen were now walking back toward their machine, clearly satisfied with what they had done. Even at this distance, one could see that they were happy and relaxed

—perhaps for the first time since they had reached Thalassa. The water to rebuild the *Magellan's* shield was on its way out into space, to be shaped and frozen by the other strange forces that these men had made their servants. In a few days, they would be ready to leave, their great interstellar ark as good as new.

Even until this minute, Lora had hoped that they might fail. There was nothing left of that hope now, as she watched the man-made waterspout lift its burden from the sea. Sometimes it wavered slightly, its base shifting back and forth as if at the balance point between immense and invisible forces. But it was fully under control, and it would do the task that had been set for it. That meant only one thing to her; soon she must say good-by to Leon.

She walked slowly toward the distant group of Earthmen, marshaling her thoughts and trying to subdue her emotions. Presently Leon broke away from his friends and came to meet her; relief and happiness were written across his face, but they faded swiftly when he saw Lora's expression.

"Well," he said lamely, almost like a schoolboy caught in some crime, "we've done it."

"And now—how long will you be here?"

He scuffed nervously at the sand, unable to meet her eye.

"Oh, about three days—perhaps four."

She tried to assimilate the words calmly; after all, she had expected them—this was nothing new. But she failed completely, and it was as well that there was no one near them.

"You can't leave!" she cried desperately. "Stay here on Thalassa!"

Leon took her hands gently, then murmured: "No, Lora—this isn't my world; I would never fit into it. Half my life's been spent training for the work I'm doing now; I could never be happy here, where there aren't any more frontiers. In a month I should die of boredom."

"Then take me with you!"

"You don't really mean that."

"But I do!"

"You only think so; you'd be more out of place in my world than I would be in yours."

"I could learn—there would be plenty of things I could do. As long as we could stay together!"

He held her at arm's length, looking into her eyes. They mirrored sorrow, and also sincerity. She really believed what she was saying, Leon told himself. For the first time, his conscience smote him. He had forgotten—or chosen not to remember—how much more serious these things could be to a woman than to a man.

He had never intended to hurt Lora; he was very fond of her, and would remember her with affection all his life. Now he was discovering, as so many men before him had done, that it was not always easy to say good-by.

There was only one thing to do. Better a short, sharp pain than a long bitterness.

"Come with me, Lora," he said. "I have something to show you."

They did not speak as Leon led the way to the clearing that the Earthmen used as a landing ground. It was littered with pieces of enigmatic equipment, some of them being repacked while others were being left behind for the islanders to use as they pleased. Several of the antigravity scooters were parked in the shade beneath the palms; even when not in use they spurned contact with the ground, and hovered a couple of feet above the grass.

But it was not these that Leon was interested in; he walked purposefully toward the gleaming oval that dominated the clearing, and spoke a few words to the engineer who was standing beside it. There was a short argument; then the other capitulated with fairly good grace.

"It's not fully loaded," Leon explained as he helped Lora up the ramp. "But we're going just the same. The other shuttle will be down in half an hour, anyway."

Already Lora was in a world she had never known before—a world of technology in which the most brilliant engineer or scientist of Thalassa would be lost. The island possessed all the machines it needed for its life and happiness; this was something utterly beyond its ken. Lora had once seen the great computer that was the virtual ruler of her people and with whose decisions they disagreed not once in a generation. That giant brain was huge and complex, but there was an awesome simplicity about this machine that impressed even her nontechnical mind. When Leon sat down at the absurdly small control board, his hands seemed to do nothing except rest lightly upon it.

Yet the walls were suddenly transparent—and there was Thalassa, already shrinking below them. There had been no sense of movement, no whisper of sound, yet the island was dwindling even as she watched. The misty edge of the world, a great bow dividing the blue of the sea from the velvet blackness of space, was becoming more curved with every passing second.

"Look," said Leon, pointing to the stars.

The ship was already visible, and Lora felt a sudden sense of disappointment that it was so small. She could see a cluster of portholes around the center section, but there appeared to be no other breaks anywhere on the vessel's squat and angular hull.

The illusion lasted only for a second. Then, with a shock of incredulity that made her senses reel and brought her to the edge of vertigo, she saw how hopelessly her eyes had been deceived. Those were not portholes; the ship was still miles away. What she was seeing were the gaping hatches through which the ferries could shuttle on their journeys between the starship and Thalassa.

There is no sense of perspective in space, where all objects are still clear and sharp whatever their distance. Even when the hull of the ship was looming up beside them, an endless curving wall of metal eclipsing the stars, there was still no real way of judging its size. She could only guess that it must be at least two miles in length.

The ferry berthed itself, as far as Lora could judge, without any intervention from Leon. She followed him out of the little control room, and when the air lock opened she was surprised to discover that they could step directly into one of the starship's passageways.

They were standing in a long tubular corridor that stretched in each direction as far as the eye could see. The floor was moving beneath their feet, carrying them along swiftly and effortlessly—yet strangely enough Lora had felt no sudden jerk as she stepped onto the conveyer that was now sweeping her through the ship. One more mystery she would never explain; there would be many others before Leon had finished showing her the *Magellan*.

It was an hour before they met another human being. In that time they must have traveled miles, sometimes being carried along by the moving corridors, sometimes being lifted up long tubes within which gravity had been abolished. It was obvious what Leon was trying to do; he was attempting to give her some faint impression of the size and complexity of this artificial world that had been built to carry the seeds of a new civilization to the stars.

The engine room alone, with its sleeping, shrouded monsters of metal and crystal, must have been half a mile in length. As they stood on the balcony high above that vast arena of latent power, Leon said proudly, and perhaps not altogether accurately: "These are mine." Lora looked down on the huge and meaningless shapes that had carried Leon to her across the light-years, and did not know whether to bless them for what they had brought or to curse them for what they might soon take away.

They sped swiftly through cavernous holds, packed with all the machines and instruments and stores needed to mold a virgin planet and to make it a fit home for humanity. There were miles upon miles of storage racks, holding in tape or microfilm or still more compact form the cultural heritage of mankind. Here they met a group of experts from Thalassa, looking rather dazed, trying to decide how much of all this wealth they could loot in the few hours left to them.

Had her own ancestors, Lora wondered, been so well equipped when they crossed space? She doubted it; their ship had been far smaller, and Earth must have learned much about the techniques of interstellar colonization in the centuries since Thalassa was opened up. When the *Magellan*'s sleeping travelers reached their new home, their success was assured if their spirit matched their material resources.

Now they had come to a great white door which slid silently open as they approached, to reveal—of all incongruous things to find inside a spaceship—a cloakroom in which lines of heavy furs hung from pegs. Leon helped Lora to climb into one of these, then selected another for himself. She followed him uncomprehendingly as he walked toward a circle of frosted glass set in the floor; then he turned to her and said: "There's no gravity where we're going now, so keep close to me and do exactly as I say."

The crystal trap door swung upward like an opening watch glass, and out of the depths swirled a blast of cold such as Lora had never imagined, still less experienced. Thin wisps of moisture condensed in the freezing air, dancing around her like ghosts. She looked at Leon as if to say, "Surely you don't expect me to go down *there!*"

He took her arm reassuringly and said, "Don't worry— you won't notice the cold after a few minutes. I'll go first."

The trap door swallowed him; Lora hesitated for a moment, then lowered herself after him. *Lowered?* No; that was the wrong word; up and down no longer existed here. Gravity had been abolished—she was floating without weight in this frigid, snow-white universe. All around her were glittering honeycombs of glass, forming thousands and tens of thousands of hexagonal cells. They were laced together with clusters of pipes and bundles of wiring, and each cell was large enough to hold a human being.

And each cell did. There they were, sleeping all around her, the thousands of colonists to whom Earth was still, in literal truth, a memory of yesterday. What were they dreaming, less than halfway through their three-hundred-year sleep? Did the brain dream at all in this dim no man's land between life and death?

Narrow, endless belts, fitted with handholds every few feet, were strung across the face of the honeycomb. Leon grabbed one of these, and let it tow them swiftly past the great mosaic of hexagons. Twice they changed direction, switching from one belt to another, until at last they must have been a full quarter of a mile from the point where they had started.

Leon released his grip, and they drifted to rest beside one cell no different from all the myriads of others. But as Lora saw the expression on Leon's face, she knew why he had brought her here, and knew that her battle was already lost.

The girl floating in her crystal coffin had a face that was not beautiful, but was full of character and intelligence. Even in this centuries-long repose, it showed determination and resourcefulness. It was the face of a pioneer, of a frontierswoman who could stand beside her mate and help him wield whatever fabulous tools of science might be neeeded to build a new Earth beyond the stars.

For a long time, unconscious of the cold, Lora stared down at the sleeping rival who would never know of her existence. Had any love, she wondered, in the whole history of the world, ever ended in so strange a place?

At last she spoke, her voice hushed as if she feared to wake these slumbering legions.

"Is she your wife?"

Leon nodded.

"I'm sorry, Lora. I never intended to hurt you. . . ."

"It doesn't matter now. It was my fault, too." She paused, and looked more closely at the sleeping woman. "And your child as well?"

"Yes; it will be born three months after we land."

How strange to think of a gestation that would last nine months and three hundred years! Yet it was all part of the same pattern; and that, she knew now, was a pattern that had no place for her.

These patient multitudes would haunt her dreams for the rest of her life; as the crystal trap door closed behind her, and warmth crept back into her body, she wished that the cold that had entered her heart could be so easily dispelled. One day, perhaps, it would be; but many days and many lonely nights must pass ere that time came.

She remembered nothing of the journey back through the labyrinth of corridors and echoing chambers; it took her by surprise when she found herself once more in the cabin of the little ferry ship that had brought them up from Thalassa. Leon walked over to the controls, made a few adjustments, but did not sit down.

"Good-by, Lora," he said. "My work is done. It would be better if I stayed here." He took her hands in his; and now, in the last moment they would ever have together, there were no words that she could say. She could not even see his face for the tears that blurred her vision.

His hands tightened once, then relaxed. He gave a strangled sob, and when she could see clearly again, the cabin was empty.

A long time later a smooth, synthetic voice announced from the control board, "We have landed; please leave by the forward air lock," The pattern of opening doors guided her steps, and presently she was looking out into the busy clearing she had left a lifetime ago.

A small crowd was watching the ship with attentive interest, as if had not landed a hundred times before. For a moment she did not understand the reason; then Clyde's voice roared, "Where is he? I've had enough of this!"

In a couple of bounds he was up the ramp and had gripped her roughly by the arm. "Tell him to come out like a man!"

Lora shook her head listlessly.

"He's not here," she answered. "I've said good-by to him. I'll never see him again."

Clyde stared at her disbelievingly, then saw that she spoke the truth. In the same moment she crumbled into his arms, sobbing as if her heart would break. As she collapsed, his anger, too, collapsed within him, and all that he had intended to say to her vanished from his mind. She belonged to him again; there was nothing else that mattered now.

For almost fifty hours the geyser roared off the coast of Thalassa, until its work was done. All the island watched, through the lenses of the television cameras, the shaping of the iceberg that would ride ahead of the *Magellan* on her way to the stars. May the new shield serve her better, prayed all who watched, than the one she had brought from Earth. The great cone of ice was itself protected, during these few hours while it was close to Thalassa's sun, by a paper-thin screen of polished metal that kept it always in shadow. The sunshade would be left behind as soon as the journey began; it would not be needed in the interstellar wastes.

The last day came and went; Lora's heart was not the only one to feel sadness now as the sun went down and the men from Earth made their final farewells to the world they would never forget—and which their sleeping friends would never remember. In the same swift silence with which it had first landed, the gleaming egg lifted from the clearing, dipped for a moment in salutation above the village, and climbed back into its natural element. Then Thalassa waited.

The night was shattered by a soundless detonation of light. A point of pulsing brilliance no larger than a single star had banished all the hosts of heaven and now dominated the sky, far outshining the pale disk of Selene and casting sharp-edged shadows on the ground—shadows that moved even as one watched. Up there on the borders of space the fires that powered the suns themselves were burning now, preparing to drive the starship out into immensity on the last leg of her interrupted journey.

Dry-eyed, Lora watched the silent glory on which half her heart was riding out toward the stars. She was drained of emotion now; if she had tears, they would come later.

Was Leon already sleeping or was he looking back upon Thalassa, thinking of what might have been? Asleep or waking, what did it matter now. . . ?

She felt Clyde's arms close around her, and welcomed their comfort against the loneliness of space. This was where she belonged; her heart would not stray again. *Good-by, Leon —may you be happy on that far world which you and your children will conquer for mankind. But think of me sometimes, two hundred years behind you on the road to Earth.*

She turned her back upon the blazing sky and buried her face in the shelter of Clyde's arms. He stroked her hair with clumsy gentleness, wishing that he had words to comfort her yet knowing that silence was best. He felt no sense of victory; though Lora was his once more, their old and innocent companionship was gone beyond recall. Leon's memory would fade, but it would never wholly die. All the days of his life, Clyde knew, the ghost of Leon would come between him and Lora—the ghost of a man who would be not one day older when they lay in their graves.

The light was fading from the sky as the fury of the star drive dwindled along its lonely and unreturning road. Only once did Lora turn away from Clyde to look again at the departing ship. Its journey had scarcely begun, yet already it was moving across the heavens more swiftly than any meteor; in a few moments it would have fallen below the edge of the horizon as it plunged past the orbit of Thalassa, beyond the barren outer planets, and on into the abyss.

She clung fiercely to the strong arms that enfolded her, and felt against her cheek the beating of Clyde's heart—

the heart that belonged to her and which she would never spurn again. Out of the silence of the night there came a sudden, long-drawn sigh from the watching thousands, and she knew that the *Magellan* had sunk out of sight below the edge of the world. It was all over.

She looked up at the empty sky to which the stars were now returning—the stars which she could never see again without remembering Leon. But he had been right; that way was not for her. She knew now, with a wisdom beyond her years, that the starship *Magellan* was outward bound into history; and that was something of which Thalassa had no further part. Her world's story had begun and ended with the pioneers three hundred years ago, but the colonists of the *Magellan* would go on to victories and achievements as great as any yet written in the sagas of mankind. Leon and his companions would be moving seas, leveling mountains, and conquering unknown perils when her descendants eight generations hence would still be dreaming beneath the sun-soaked palms.

And which was better, who could say?

More SIGNET Books by Robert A. Heinlein

| | | |
|---|---|---|
| ☐ | **ASSIGNMENT IN ETERNITY** | (#J9360—$1.95) |
| ☐ | **BEYOND THIS HORIZON** | (#J9833—$1.95) |
| ☐ | **THE DAY AFTER TOMORROW** | (#W7766—$1.50) |
| ☐ | **THE DOOR INTO SUMMER** | (#J9628—$1.95) |
| ☐ | **DOUBLE STAR** | (#E8905—$1.75) |
| ☐ | **THE GREEN HILLS OF EARTH** | (#J9952—$1.95) |
| ☐ | **THE MAN WHO SOLD THE MOON** | (#J8717—$1.95) |
| ☐ | **THE MENACE FROM EARTH** | (#E9870—$2.25) |
| ☐ | **METHUSELAH'S CHILDREN** | (#E9875—$2.25) |
| ☐ | **THE PUPPET MASTERS** | (#AJ1188—$1.95) |
| ☐ | **WALDO & MAGIC, INC.** | (#J9754—$1.95) |

Buy them at your local

bookstore or use coupon

on next page for ordering.

## SIGNET Books You'll Enjoy

☐ **TRIPLE by Ken Follett.** (#E9447—$3.50)

☐ **EYE OF THE NEEDLE by Ken Follett.** (#E9550—$3.50)

☐ **THE REVENANT by Brana Lobel.** (#E9451—$2.25)*

☐ **THE BLACK HORDE by Richard Lewis.** (#E9454—$1.75)

☐ **A FEAST FOR SPIDERS by Kenneth L. Evans.**
(#J9484—$1.95)*

☐ **THE DARK by James Herbert.** (#E9403—$2.95)

☐ **THE DEATH MECHANIC by A. D. Hutter.** (#J9410—$1.95)*

☐ **THE MAGNATE by Jack Mayfield.** (#E9411—$2.25)*

☐ **THE SURROGATE by Nick Sharman.** (#E9293—$2.50)*

☐ **THE SCOURGE by Nick Sharman.** (#E9114—$2.25)*

☐ **INTENSIVE FEAR by Nick Christian.** (#E9341—$2.25)*

☐ **AUCTION! by Tom Murphy.** (#E9478—$2.95)

☐ **ELISE by Sara Reavin.** (#E9483—$2.95)

☐ **HAWK OF MAY by Gillian Bradshaw.** (#E9765—$2.75)*

☐ **GAMEMAKER by David Cohter.** (#E9766—$2.50)*

☐ **CUBAN DEATH-LIFT (3rd in the MacMorgan series) by Randy Striker.** (#J9768—$1.95)*

* Price slightly higher in Canada

---